THE REDHEAD
FROM SUN DOG

Center Point
Large Print

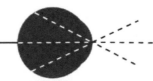

**This Large Print Book carries the
Seal of Approval of N.A.V.H.**

THE REDHEAD FROM SUN DOG

W. C. TUTTLE

CENTER POINT LARGE PRINT
THORNDIKE, MAINE

This Center Point Large Print edition
is published in the year 2012 by arrangement with
Golden West Literary Agency.

First US edition: Houghton Mifflin
First UK edition: Collins

The text of this Large Print edition is unabridged.
In other aspects, this book may vary
from the original edition.
Printed in the United States of America
on permanent paper.
Set in 16-point Times New Roman type.

ISBN: 978-1-61173-591-8

Library of Congress Cataloging-in-Publication Data

Tuttle, W. C. (Wilbur C.), 1883–1969.
 The redhead from sun dog / W. C. Tuttle.
 pages ; cm.
 ISBN 978-1-61173-591-8 (library binding : alk. paper)
 1. Large type books. I. Title.
 PS3539.U988R43 2012
 813′.52—dc23
                                              2012029963

CONTENTS

THE REDHEAD
FROM SUN DOG

CHAPTER I

THE REDHEAD SETS A PRECEDENT

". . . HANGED by the neck until you are dead—
and may the Lord have mercy on your soul."

Old Judge Wetherby's voice broke on the last
word, but he shut his lips tightly, swallowed
thickly, and blinked around the courtroom, like
an old owl, suddenly awakened in broad daylight. It was the first time in his life that he had
ever been obliged to pronounce the sentence of
death.

There was not another sound in the courtroom.
It was like a creaky old phonograph talking in a
deserted house. One could almost imagine the
scratching of the needle, but it was only one of
the judge's cuff links, scraping on the old desk-
top.

"Silent" Slade, the prisoner, towering six feet,
four inches, stood facing the old judge; a giant,
with somber brown eyes in a huge face, looking
at the little old man who had doomed him to die.
Not a muscle twitched in the big man's face as he
turned his head and looked at the crowded courtroom, but he was seeing them through a haze.

Just behind Silent Slade stood "Brick" Davidson,
the sheriff of Sun Dog County. Brick was of
medium height, wiry of build, and with a thatch

9

of flaming red. His thin face was plentifully sprinkled with freckles, but he was so pale now that they didn't show. Brick looked old and drawn; a tired old man at thirty years of age.

The law had decreed that his best friend must die, and he—Brick Davidson, the sheriff—must perform the execution. He didn't look at Silent. He wondered how in the world the pit of his stomach could get so far away from him. One time he had gone down fifteen stories in a swift elevator, and the feeling was almost the same. Suddenly he was conscious of the booming voice of Silent Slade, a decided contrast to the rasping, high-pitched voice of the old judge:

"Well, pardner, I reckon we might as well go back and finish that seven-up game."

Brick looked up quickly. Silent had turned and was looking at him, a whimsical smile on his wide mouth. It broke the tension of the courtroom. Men began to shuffle their feet, as they walked out, looking back at the red-headed sheriff and his condemned prisoner. The old judge hurried out, walking in short, jerky steps. Some women stopped at the doorway and looked back. One woman was crying. She was Mrs. Cale Wesson, a big, motherly sort.

She loved both Brick and Silent in a motherly way; had known them for years.

"As if your tears would do any good!" said a woman.

Mrs. Wesson turned and went down the stairs. Brick put his hand on Silent's arm and they went down the back stairs and around to the little jail.

"Want to play now?" asked Brick hoarsely.

Silent shook his head. "I reckon I'd rather set down and think for a while, pardner."

"Damn it, I don't want to think!" said Brick savagely, striking the bars with an open palm. "I don't never want to think ag'in."

"Well, you've got more time than I have—you can wait."

"Rub it in!" wailed Brick. "Ain'tcha got no feelin's, Silent?"

"Yo're funny," sighed Silent. "You act almost as though you was the one who was goin' to git hanged."

"I'd jist as soon. By God, I'd rather!"

Brick turned and walked down the narrow corridor; here he entered his office.

"Soapy" Caswell, a typical old cattleman, as gray as a badger, and with a hair-trigger disposition, was tilted back against the wall, his boot-heels hooked over a rung. Soapy was a big man in Sun Dog. He owned the Marlin City Bank, was heavily interested in the banks at Silverton and Redrock, and also owned the Circle Cross Ranch.

Soapy was keen-minded, had plenty of money, and was beginning to be a power in politics. He had watched Brick Davidson grow up in Sun

Dog, and he was personally interested in seeing Brick go beyond what county politics might offer.

Brick had been a top-hand cowboy before he became sheriff. He was a square-shooter, a fighter; a born leader, unless Soapy was mistaken. There had never been any affection between Soapy and Brick. They quarreled very often, and Soapy liked Brick for his independence.

Brick tossed his hat on a desk and sat down wearily. Soapy squinted at him, but said nothing for a while. Finally he cleared his throat.

"How'd yuh like to go to the State Senate, Brick?" he asked.

Brick looked at him, but didn't answer. In fact, he hardly heard what Soapy had said.

"I've been thinkin' it over," said Soapy. "The election ain't more than three months away. You've made a good sheriff—a danged good one. You've made a lot of friends; friends that'll back yuh in anythin'. I'd like to see yuh nominated for the State Senate. It's a steppin'-stone. You've got to git before the public, Brick. I'll betcha that if yuh do go to the Senate, it won't be more'n four years before you'll carry this State for United States Senate. Yo're a fighter. The Lord knows this State needs a fighter."

Soapy stopped to let his words soak in.

"Were you in the courthouse?" asked Brick.

"Yeah, I was there."

"Then you ought to know how much I'm interested in you, Soapy."

"That's the risk yuh took, when yuh accepted that office—havin' to hang yore friends. I like Silent. But that ain't got a thing to do with it. Silent murdered a man."

"Did he?" asked Brick wearily.

"Twelve men said he did. They was only out fifteen minutes. If I'd 'a' been on that jury, they'd 'a' been 'hung' yet. Where's Harp?"

Harp Harris was Brick's deputy. He was six feet, two inches tall, thin as a rail, and with a long, lean face, which registered deep despair most of the time.

"Harp's sufferin' from tonsillitis, and he's home with his wife," said Brick dully. "And he's also a damn liar. He don't even know where his tonsils are. All's the matter with him was that he didn't want to be in the courthouse this mornin'. Della came down and told me about it. She said he was sufferin'. I s'pose he was; so was I."

"It makes a tough job for you," said Soapy. "But you won't resign."

"How do yuh know I won't?"

"Because I know you, Brick."

"I'm the kind of a feller who'd hang a friend, eh?"

"Yo're the kind of a man who obeys the letter of the law."

13

"You better get to hell out of here, before I kick yuh out, Soapy."

"You and what other six big men?" belligerently.

Brick shook his head despondently.

"Soapy, I want to do the right thing. Could you hang yore best friend? Me and Silent have bunked together, rode together, fought together. We've split fifty-fifty on everythin'. Silent is as square as a dollar. I don't care a damn what that jury said. Silent told me he never did shoot Scotty McKee, and I believe him. I'm no judge nor jury, of course. And now I've got to hang him. Got to trip that damn trap and—and murder my best friend."

"Hangin' ain't murder, Brick."

"It's legal murder."

"All right. I never made the law, and I don't believe in it any more than you do. Now that we've settled all that, how do yuh feel about runnin' for the State Senate?"

"No money in it."

"That's plenty true—but it advertises yuh. Listen to me: I've got money. I've got friends who have money. There's certain things that this State needs, and it'll take National legislation to get it. We need a man with guts enough to go after it; sabe? There's a machine in this State that needs bustin', and we're startin' in to forge a monkey-wrench to throw into their cog-wheels. The State Senate don't pay yuh much, but here's

14

what I'll do; I'll make yuh foreman of the Circle Cross, with time off to be a Senator. Think it over, Brick. I ain't said a word to anybody—yet. But I can swing a lot of money over to my way of thinkin'. Damn it, I want to make somethin' out of yuh!"

"Why?"

"I knowed you'd ask that. Mebby I've got an axe to grind. Mebby you'd make a lot of money for me. And mebby it's because I never had any son of my own. I'm gettin' old, Brick—old and foolish. I'd like to see yuh go high in the world—and know I helped yuh there."

Soapy tilted forward in his chair, got to his feet, and walked outside, without saying anything more.

"Danged old pelican!" breathed Brick softly, as he sagged forward, holding his head in his hands. He wanted to think—and it was not about Soapy and his plans. Think! That was all he had been doing since the day he had been forced to arrest Silent Slade for the murder of Scotty McKee.

Scotty McKee had come to Marlin City a year previous to his murder, and had purchased the Nine Bar Nine cattle outfit from Lafe Freeman. McKee paid cash, and old Lafe had retired to a single room in the Marlin City Hotel, where he could sit all day on a sidewalk, whittle, chew tobacco, and play a little poker.

Little was known about McKee, except that he

came from somewhere down along the Mexican Border. He had been on the ranch about two months when his daughter came from school in San Francisco and joined him. She was twenty years of age, a tall, dark-eyed girl, who had turned the head of Silent Slade, who had never had a girl before.

McKee was a silent sort of a person, sticking fairly close to work and rarely coming to town. Juanita was a good dancer, and was so much in demand that Silent was often plunged in the depths of despair. She told Silent that her mother had been a Spaniard. She and her father talked Spanish together, which caused Silent to purchase a Spanish-English dictionary. He threw it away in a few days, after Juanita promised to teach him the language.

Six months after Juanita came to Marlin City, Silent went to work for her father. He and "Banty" Harrison were the only help employed, as Scotty McKee was able to do much of his own work. Silent was in the seventh heaven. It gave him a chance to be near Juanita.

There had never been any engagement, but Silent took it for granted that Juanita would marry him. But Scotty McKee evidently had different plans for Juanita, and he told her so in no uncertain terms. She told Silent what her father had said, and he decided to settle the issue by a single-handed debate with Scotty McKee.

It was on a Saturday, when Scotty ordered Banty to hitch up the buggy team and take Juanita to Silverton to do some shopping. He told Silent to take the day off, if he wanted to—which he did. Juanita decided to do her shopping in Marlin City, which gave Banty a good opportunity to quench his thirst while Silent took care of Juanita.

There was nothing wrong in this. A woman is privileged to change her mind as often as she wishes—and Juanita was a woman. It was about four o'clock in the afternoon when Juanita decided to go home, and, strangely enough, Banty was still able to drive a team.

Silent rode away ahead of them, determined to have it out with Scotty McKee before Juanita came back to the ranch. And that was where Silent Slade made a mistake. He testified on the witness stand that he rode to the ranch, and that he thought he heard a shot fired while he was at the stable putting up his horse.

He said he went to the front door of the house and found it locked. Then he went around the west side of the house, where he found a window open. He heard somebody moving around in there, decided that it was McKee, and went back to the front door, where he knocked heavily, but there was no response.

Then he sat down on the porch. He said he had no suspicion of anything wrong. There were a number of calves in the big corral, ready for the branding-iron, and, as he sat there on the porch, a coyote crossed an open spot below the corral. He said he drew out his six-shooter and fired a shot at the coyote, which caused the animal to leave that vicinity at top speed.

He did not see Juanita and Banty nearing the ranch, but went back to the open window, wondering where Scotty McKee might be. Finally he crawled through the window, and he said there was a decided odor of burned powder. In the living-room of the ranch house he found Scotty McKee, lying on his face in the middle of the room, shot through the heart.

Silent said he turned McKee over and examined him. Banty testified that he knocked on the front door, but Silent says he never heard it. And then, rather dazed by the tragedy, Silent went back to the open window and crawled out of the house, instead of unlocking the front door, and both Juanita and Banty saw him crawling out.

The prosecution based their case on three facts: that Scotty McKee had never had any trouble with any one in Sun Dog County; that he had refused to sanction the marriage of Juanita and Silent Slade, and Silent had gone out there, looking for a showdown; and that Silent had crawled through a window, getting away from the scene of the crime, instead of going out through the door.

Juanita refused to testify, except at the coroner's inquest, where she was still too dazed to understand what the public thought about it. Banty testified to the facts as he knew them. Silent had told him he was going out to have a showdown with Scotty McKee; which didn't help Silent any. The shot at the coyote, whether mythical or not, helped the prosecution, because Silent had neglected to remove the empty cartridge from his gun, and McKee had been shot with the same caliber gun as the one used by Silent Slade.

Silent stuck doggedly to his first story, and all the efforts of the prosecution failed to change it in any way. Juanita was heartbroken over the affair and stayed close to the ranch. Brick had worked on the case from every angle, trying to find some clue which might help Silent Slade. Juanita seemed to know little about her father's business. He had kept her in school, supplied her with money, and she had never really become acquainted with her father until they came to the Sun Dog country.

On the day that Scotty McKee had been shot, Brick found two things at the ranch house near the body. One was an old envelope, partly covered with penciled figures, addressed to Jim Breen, Gomez Springs, Mexico. The other was an old Bull Durham tobacco sack, containing a little marahuana weed. Brick didn't know what the stuff was until he sent it to a drug company for analysis.

Marahuana is really a Mexican product, although it is grown secretly in places in the Southwest, and the dried leaves are mixed with tobacco in cigarettes. Its use apparently destroys the smoker's ideas of right and wrong, and an overdose is said to be conducive to homicide. Scotty McKee had been a big, husky sort of a man, who drank but little and smoked none.

Brick knew that Banty Harrison did not own the stuff, nor did Silent Slade. Brick asked Juanita about the name on the envelope, but she did not know any Jim Breen. But she did know that the penciled figures on the envelope had not been made by her father.

Juanita didn't know where her father had made his money. He had told her a little of a cattle ranch near the Border, but had mentioned no names or places—and that Border is around fourteen hundred miles in length.

Brick had talked with the prosecutor about the envelope and the marahuana weed; but the prosecutor was little interested. He was looking for a conviction, not clues to ruin his case against Slade. The court appointed a lawyer from Silverton to defend Silent, but as a defense it was a mere matter of form. Silent had one story to tell, and the jury didn't believe it.

Brick's mind was wandering back over the

evidence, when "Harp" Harris, his deputy, came slowly into the office from the street. Harp's long neck was encompassed in a red woolen sock, which sagged away from his prominent Adam's apple and gave off an unmistakable odor of liniment.

"How'd he stand it?" asked Harp huskily. Brick looked up at him.

"Who do yuh mean?"

"Silent."

"Oh!" softly. "I didn't know yuh was interested."

"You know that's a lie, Brick. I've been awful sick, I tell yuh. Della didn't want me to come out now. Damn it, she's settin' around the house bawlin' right now."

"About you comin' out in the open with a sock on the wrong end of yuh?"

"No—about what they're goin' to do to Silent."

"What they're goin' to do, eh? Didja ever stop to think that 'they' are me and you, Harp? That's our job."

"Not me! I resign right now."

"No, yuh won't. You quit me now, and I'll make a widow out of yore wife. Harp, I think I'll resign and make you sheriff."

"Make me—" an expression of panic flashed across Harp's lean face. "No, yuh don't! Nossir! Don't do that. I'll resign, if yuh do."

"You'd make a good sheriff for Sun Dog."

"Shore, I would, unless somethin' serious came up before I could git my resignation wrote out."

21

"I guess we're a hell of a pair of officers," sighed Brick.

"I dunno about you—but I'm offerin' no defense for my end of it. I reckon I'll go back and talk with Silent."

"Go ahead. Yo're about as cheerful as an undertaker. If I was goin' to git hung, I'd welcome you, Harp; that expression on yore face would make most anythin' welcome."

"I tell yuh, I'm sick."

"So am I, but I don't need any sock around my neck."

Brick left the office and walked up to the bank, where he wrote out a check for a hundred dollars and cashed it. When he left there he met the prosecuting attorney.

"I suppose you know that the county allows you enough money to employ two additional deputies until after the execution," he said. "In a case of this kind it is customary to keep the prisoner under constant surveillance."

Brick nodded slowly.

"I'll pick me a couple men to-morrow."

"Be sure and get men you can trust, Sheriff. Slade is well liked."

"I realize that."

"Makes it rather difficult for you, I guess."

"Oh, I'll get along."

"Certainly you will. This is really a supreme test of a man's nerve."

Brick looked queerly at him, but did not reply. In front of the office he met Harp.

"Didja have a nice visit with Silent?" asked Brick.

"Fine," said Harp thickly. "I said hello, Silent, and he said hello, Harp, and then we set there and looked at each other. After while I says so-long, Silent, and he says so-long, Harp. Yea-a-ah, it was a fine visit. How do I go about quittin' my job?"

"Better wait a while," advised Brick. "You've got a wife to support, and yuh don't want to go back to forty a month, do yuh?"

"Della said I ort to quit."

"Ask her to subtract forty from a hundred and ten, and see the difference. And yuh might not be able to even get a job punchin' cows at forty a month. And if anythin' happened to me, you'd be the sheriff and draw about three hundred a month."

"You ain't figurin' on anythin' happenin' to yuh, are yuh?"

"In the midst of life, we are in death," grinned Brick.

"That's right—yuh never can tell. Lincoln's dead and Washington's dead—and I don't feel so damn well m'self. Well, I'll go and gurgle m' neck some more. Yuh won't need me no more to-day, will yuh?"

"Didn't need yuh at all, as far as that's concerned."

23

"Thank yuh kindly. I'll be all right to-morrow, Brick."

"Yuh may be well, but you'll never be all right."

It was part of Harp's duties to feed prisoners, and Brick was eating his breakfast in the little restaurant the following morning when Harp came in, half-running in his haste, carrying his hat in his hand.

"The jail has been busted!" he blurted out. "Silent's gone!"

Brick got quickly to his feet. There were a number of men in the restaurant, and they all left their meals to follow down to the jail. Word spread quickly that Silent Slade had escaped, and the curious came to see how the jail break had been accomplished.

Five of the bars had been cut through and bent aside. Once into the corridor, it was easy enough for the prisoner to get out of the main building, as the doors were locked with a spring. Harp also discovered that Brick's horse and saddle were missing, and that Silent's six-shooter had been taken from a drawer of the sheriff's desk, along with a new box of cartridges.

The prosecuting attorney had been quickly advised of the escape, and was down there within a few minutes, examining the cut bars. Sun Dog County's jail was of rather an ancient vintage, and the bars, instead of being tempered steel, were rather soft iron.

The prosecuting attorney looked the cuts over critically. He even shut the door of the cell and tried to crawl out through the twisted bars.

"Rather queer," he observed to the crowd. "Slade is a much larger man than I am, and it is impossible for me to get out. Do any of you know whether Slade was right- or left-handed?"

"Right-handed," said Harp quickly.

"That's rather queer. If you will notice closely, these bars have all been cut from the left side, and the cut has a downward tendency. It is easy to prove which side the cut was made, as the last fraction of an inch of the bar was broken off, not sawed. Either Slade is left-handed or those bars were cut from outside."

The attorney turned and looked squarely at Brick.

"What are *you* going to do about it?" he asked.

Not a muscle of Brick's face moved, and his eyes were level as he looked squarely at the lawyer.

"I might ask the county to replace them bars with steel ones. It will make it easier for the man who gets my job."

Brick turned on his heel and walked out to his office, where he sat down and wrote out his resignation. The crowd filed out through the office, leaving Harp and Brick together.

"Did that maverick mean to insinuate that you turned Silent loose?" asked Harp angrily. "If he did, I'll—"

"Keep yore shirt on," advised Brick. He finished writing, placed the letter in an envelope and addressed it to the County Commissioners of Sun Dog County.

"Take this over to the courthouse," he ordered Harp. "I've advised that you be sworn in at once, so that yuh can get on the trail of Silent Slade."

"Brick, you ain't resignin'!"

"Yeah, I've resigned. Yuh see, I never thought about Silent bein' right-handed, and I never thought about him not bein' able to crawl out through them bars."

"Hey, Brick! What's all this I'm hearin'?"

Soapy Caswell stumbled through the doorway, carrying his hat in his hand. "Some of them danged fools said"—he stopped for breath— "said that you—you let Silent Slade get away."

"I heard that's what they're sayin', Soapy. I've just written out my resignation."

"You've written—Brick, are yuh goin' to let them loud-mouthed jiggers get away with anythin' like that? You never let him loose! They said that the bars was sawed. My God, what do they want? Brick, you can't do this. With the reputation you've got—and what's ahead of yuh. Why don'tcha say somethin'?"

"Would yuh mind deliverin' that letter, Harp?"

"Oh, shore."

Harp went away, shaking his head.

"Now, *you* do a little talkin'," urged Soapy.

"I haven't anythin' to say. I reckon you've heard it all, anyway."

"Brick, yo're ruined, as far as politics are concerned. This story will go everywhere. Sheriff's bunkie sentenced to hang and is turned loose by the sheriff. My God, can yuh imagine how that will look to folks?"

"I thought it all out, Soapy."

"You gave him a horse and saddle and his gun."

"And a hundred dollars for expenses," said Brick calmly. "He's got to eat."

"Yo're a hell of a sheriff!"

"I know it—and I'm sorry, Soapy. The prosecutin' attorney is mad enough to eat spikes. Dang him, he got his conviction, what more does he want?"

"Does he know you've resigned?"

"Prob'ly does by this time."

Soapy chuckled softly for a moment.

"He'll shore raise the roof when he finds that you've resigned."

"Why?"

"Because I bet him a hundred dollars yesterday that you'd never hang Silent Slade. I'm goin' up and collect. See yuh later, Brick."

Harp came back from the courthouse. He didn't

27

find any of the Commissioners in, but he left the letter where they'd find it.

"I'm pullin' out to-night," Brick told him. "You might do a little huntin' for Silent, if they make you sheriff. And after a few days yuh might find my horse and saddle."

"Might find 'em where?"

"Oh, most any place in the County. Right now they're in yore stable. If I never come back, they're yours, Harp. Silent caught a freight train out of here last night."

"Where's he goin'?"

"I didn't ask him."

At five o'clock that afternoon Brick's resignation was still unopened on the Commissioners' desk, and Brick was packing up his few belongings. The prosecuting attorney was mad. He had paid the hundred dollars to Soapy Caswell, who was gloating considerably; but he wasn't mad about the money.

"A lovely state of affairs!" he snorted. "Murderer at large in the hills, turned loose by the sheriff, and nobody looking for him. Can you imagine such a thing. Brick Davidson should go to jail for this."

"Can yuh prove he turned Slade loose?" asked Soapy.

"Prove it! How can I prove it? Those bars have been turned around in their sockets until no man could prove from which side they had been cut;

and they've been bent back far enough to allow any man to crawl through."

"But you had witnesses to how they looked this mornin'."

"Did I? Well, I thought I did, until I questioned some of them. Fine state of affairs! He's probably had twenty hours in which to make his escape, and no warnings have been sent out. This County is without a sheriff, Mr. Caswell. For two cents I'd resign myself."

"Well," drawled Soapy, "I'll take up a collection, if yuh really feel thataway."

"Oh, you know what I mean."

"Shore."

Soapy Caswell and Harp Harris were the only ones who knew that Brick was leaving Marlin City that evening. Soapy tried to give Brick the hundred dollars he had won from the lawyer, but Brick said he had plenty of money. He and Harp shook hands silently and solemnly.

"Will yuh ever come back?" asked Harp, as the train began moving.

"Some day, Harp. Good-bye, Soapy."

"When yuh come back, bring 'em both with yuh," said Soapy.

"Both what, Soapy?"

"Silent Slade and the man who shot Scotty McKee."

Brick grinned back at them, but his heart was heavy as he watched the old town fade out in the distance. He had lived nearly all his life in Sun Dog County. His mother had died when he was ten years of age, and two years later his father died. He had been christened Arthur William Davidson, but his thatch of brick red hair had ruined Arthur William shortly after his christening.

Thrown on the world at twelve years of age, he picked up with a trail herd, heading for Montana, eventually landing in Sun Dog. And, except for a few outside trips, Brick had been in Sun Dog ever since the day he had come into the valley, trailing in the dust of a herd.

Sun Dog had never known a better sheriff than Brick Davidson. He had plenty of bullet scars to show that the job had been no sinecure. But now he had violated his oath of office, betrayed the law he had sworn to uphold.

Brick sighed deeply, as he watched the sunset fading across the Sun Dog hills. In his pocket was a ticket to San Francisco. Just why San Francisco, he didn't know, except that he had always wanted to see the old gray town on Golden Gate. The conductor interrupted his reveries.

"Takin' a trip for your health, Sheriff?"

Brick looked up quickly, recognized the conductor, and smiled thinly.

"I reckon that's what it amounts to, Carlin."

"Goin' to Frisco, eh?" looking at the strip of

30

ticket. "Well, that's fine. Just takin' a vacation or are you goin' after a prisoner?"

"I can't tell yuh—yet."

"Well, good luck to you."

"Thanks; I'll need plenty of it."

CHAPTER II

JIM BREEN

IN days gone by, the Rancho del Rosa was known far and wide in the Border country. Don Enrique Maxwell, loved and respected by every one, from sandaled friar to booted bandit, ruled the thousands of acres where his cattle roamed. Those who traveled El Camino Real found a welcome at the Rancho del Rosa, and no questions were ever asked. Don Enrique lived with an open hand, thanking God for his many blessings and the chance to help those in need.

His wife was a tall, stately Spanish woman, a daughter of the Dons, and a fit mate for Don Enrique, who was born an Englishman. They had one son, christened Roberto, a wild-riding young devil, who inherited the Rancho when his father and mother had gone the way of all flesh, married a Mexican girl, and proceeded to spend money faster than he made it.

The gambling tables called to Bob Maxwell and he answered the call, until his acres dwindled and the huge herds of cattle and horses faded away. Twenty years had passed since the Rancho had descended to Bob Maxwell. Marie, his only child, was nearly nineteen, a tall, lithe, dark-skinned beauty, educated in a Catholic school at San Francisco. She had been home less than a year, and Bob Maxwell was just beginning to realize that he had a daughter.

The buildings of the Rancho del Rosa, the Ranch of the Roses, were very old, built with thick adobe walls, deep windows, flagged walks, which the boots of caballeros and the bare feet of Indians had worn deep. Ivy covered the broad walls of the patio, mingling with the huge climbing roses which almost made a bower of the patio. In the center of the patio was the well, with its wide, low curb. Wide arches, gated with wrought iron, led from the patio to the outside.

It was only two miles to that mythical line which divided the United States from the land of mañana, unmarked, except by an occasional monument. Three miles below the line, almost due south of the Rancho, was the town of Gomez Springs.

About two miles west of the Rancho was the town of Sicomoro. It was more Mexican than American, with its adobe structures, weathered balconies, where guitars tinkled in the evenings. There were no sidewalks, and the majority of the signs were written in Spanish.

The Border Patrol had little use for Sicomoro, and Sicomoro seemed to have little use for the Border Patrol. The people of Sicomoro were close-mouthed. They told nothing. The Border Patrol swore that every man in Sicomoro was either a smuggler or a hijacker. Perhaps this was a bit exaggerated, but there had been many killings around Sicomoro, and no man had ever been brought to justice for any of them.

The Chinese population of the town fluctuated badly. At times there were only the scant dozen of regular residents, and again there might be a dozen extras. But they always left ahead of the Patrol, heading north. The several cantinas in Sicomoro did a good business in both liquor and gambling. Easy money goes quickly. Edward Pico, a swarthy son of the south, owned the liquor and gambling houses, while Wong Hop, a keen, slant-eyed son of Canton, bossed the Oriental end of the town.

It was hot down there in Sicomoro at noon time. A lone rider, tall, swarthy, slightly over-dressed, rode in on a tall sorrel and tied the animal in front of the Solo Encinas Cantina. No one knew just why it was called the Lone Oak, because there was no oak.

The sunlight glistened on his silver-mounted saddle as the animal shifted about in the yellow dust. The rider was Joe Pico, a cousin of Edward Pico, who spent much of his time in Gomez Springs. The Border Patrol was deeply suspicious of Joe, because he was apparently a leading light of Gomez Springs.

Joe accepted a drink from the bartender and sat down at a table, where three men and a dealer were playing stud poker. Joe was evidently not in the best frame of mind as he threw some silver on the table and accepted his chips. The playing was desultory, and little money changed hands. There was no conversation. Flies buzzed around the players.

A man came in and the players glanced casually at him. It was Brick Davidson, down at the heel, dusty, unshaven, but still able to grin at the world. It was two months since Brick had left Sun Dog. His blue suit was a mass of wrinkles, stained, his shirt long since ready for a laundry or a ragbag, his hat out of shape. Inside the waistband of his pants he carried a Colt revolver. He was very hot and very dusty, grateful for the coolness of the adobe cantina, with its odors of departed liquor and warm beer.

"Buenas dias," greeted the bartender.

"Yeah, I guess so," grinned Brick, leaning against the bar. "I ain't sure what it means, but that's all right, pardner."

"Have a drink?"

"I shore sabe that," grinned Brick. "Got any cold water? Yea-a-ah—water. The stuff that makes 'em build bridges. Not cold? What do you folks drink down here when yo're thirsty?"

"Mebby some tequila."

"Not with me! I drank some of that stuff about forty miles back in a town one night. I got six drinks, and woke up with five policemen on me."

"Did they put yuh in jail?"

"Five policemen?" Brick grinned scornfully. "And me with six drinks of to-kill-yuh inside? They did not. I shucked the last one off me two miles from town. No, thank yuh—no to-kill-yuh. What have we here?"

Brick walked over to the poker table and watched a few deals. He wanted to get into that game, but his finances were down to one silver dollar. Finally he addressed the dealer:

"How much does it cost to buy in on yore game, pardner?"

Brick didn't look like money to the dealer, but still another player would increase the rake-off materially. The dealer merely dealt and took the percentage, not playing himself.

"Un duro," he said, replying in Spanish.

"That's one dollar in United States," grinned Brick. "Gimme un duro's worth, will yuh?"

The dealer gave him a stack of white chips, and the game went on. Brick knew stud poker well enough to realize that a dollar's worth of chips would give him no margin for bluffing. The first pot required all his chips, but he drew out on them, winning three dollars, less the percentage, which was rather high for a small game.

But Brick wasn't kicking. His luck was with him, and inside of ten more deals he had amassed the munificent sum of twenty-five dollars, and two of the players quit the game, leaving only Joe Pico and Brick.

"If yuh want to close the game, it's all right with me," said Brick.

"That," said Pico insolently, "is an American trait."

"What's an American trait?" queried Brick.

"To quit when they're ahead of the game."

Brick's ears grew redder, a sure sign that Brick was mad, but his voice was perfectly calm, as he said:

"I ain't got no place to go, pardner; but I didn't suppose that it was worth a dealer's time to throw cards to two players."

"I am here to deal," said the man.

"Then let's play poker," grinned Brick. "I'd rather play two-handed; it only gives me one man to watch."

This time it was Pico whose ears turned red. The dealer smothered a smile. Pico had never borne a clean reputation as a gambler. Brick had enough money for a small bluff, a perfect poker face, and it was his lucky day. Pico was hot-tempered, nervous, and his eyes were an index to the cards he had drawn. Pot after pot went to Brick, while Pico smoked furiously, cursed in Spanish, and wished he had let this red-headed gringo quit while the quitting was good.

But it was too late to quit now. Brick played calmly, smiling most of the time, but watching Pico's eyes. It was not poker—it was robbery. Finally Pico sagged back in his chair, looking moodily at the table.

"Got enough?" queried Brick. "Jist quittin', or are yuh broke?"

Pico's face hardened, but he did not reply.

"I've got a couple hundred of yore money," said Brick. "Ain't yuh got no friends nor credit in this man's town? I'd like to double this amount, and what you don't know about poker would make a whoppin' big book."

Pico suddenly leaned forward.

"Just now I am short," he said coldly. "Out at the hitch-rack is my horse and saddle. I will sell both to you for one hundred and fifty dollars, if you will continue to play."

"That's a plenty money for a bronc and a hull," grinned Brick. "I'll take a look at 'em, pardner, 'cause I shore need rollin' stock."

They walked out and looked at the saddle and horse. Brick had always detested an ornamental saddle, but he could see that this one was worth many times what Pico asked for both horse and saddle, while the sorrel was a good-looking, clean-limbed animal.

"I'll stake yuh to that much," agreed Brick. "I don't like all them doo-dinguses on the saddle, but it ain't costin' me much."

They went back and resumed the game. Fortune seemed to favor Pico for a while, but Brick refused to overplay his hands. He wanted that horse and saddle, and he wanted his hundred and fifty dollars back.

Twice in a row he bluffed Pico out of a pot, accidentally turning over his hole-card and letting Pico see what he had, after the pot was won. Then came Brick's big opportunity. It had cost him fifty dollars to draw the deuce, trey, four, and five of hearts, which were in sight.

Pico's hand showed two jacks and two queens. It was foolishness on Brick's part to have stayed in the pot. Pico's eyes had showed him that he had either another jack or queen in the hole. It was Pico's bet, and he hesitated for several moments, studying Brick's cards. If Brick had either an ace or a six of hearts buried, he would have a straight flush. Brick noted the hesitancy, and said to the dealer:

"I plumb forgot to ask yuh a few questions when I horned into this game. Do yuh play straights and flushes down here?"

The dealer nodded quickly.

"And a straight flush beats four of a kind?"

"Exactly."

"That's fine," grinned Brick.

"Pass," said Pico softly, his eyes triumphant. He knew now that Brick was bluffing. And Brick seemed to be. Slowly he counted his chips and shoved them to the center. They were not many now. Pico smiled widely, as he shoved all his chips to the center.

"How can I call all that mess?" asked Brick. "I'm broke."

"You still have the horse and saddle?"

39

"That's right. We'll discount the horse a little, and I call yuh."

Swiftly Joe Pico turned over his hole-card—another jack.

"A full house," he said softly.

Brick flipped over his hole-card—the ace of hearts.

"Madre de Dios!" snorted the dealer. "A straight flush!"

Pico tried to smile, but it was a failure.

"The American don't want to quit, but he hates solitaire," said Brick seriously. "It has been a profitable day, and I'll buy a drink."

Pico drank grudgingly. He needed the drink to brace his nerves, but he didn't like to accept it from this red-headed Americano, who had the luck of the devil.

"Are you going to stay weeth us a while?" asked the dealer.

"I dunno. I'm lookin' to hook up with some cattle outfit down here. A feller was tellin' me somethin' about a ranch down here; somethin' about roses. I didn't get all of it."

"The Rancho del Rosa?"

"Shore. That's the place. This feller would say seven words in Spanish and one in English—and the English word was damn. Have another drink? No? Is there a clothin' store around here? Across the street? That's great; I shore need clothes. Well, I'll see yuh later."

Brick went striding out of the place, crossed the street, and entered a general merchandise store. Pico had several more drinks, handed out by a generous bartender.

"That man has an insulting tongue," said Pico, in Spanish.

"And a thorough knowledge of stud poker," added the dealer. "When he questioned me of the value of hands, it was for your benefit."

"Only a fool would ask a question which involved his own cards."

"That, my friend, is the secret of poker—to cause a man to believe something which is not true."

"He was insulting," persisted Pico. The several drinks of tequila were taking effect.

The dealer shrugged his shoulders.

"And the horse was worth more than I asked."

"You made the price, and he paid it."

"Dios—yes! But I was mad. I cheated myself."

"Another drink—and forget it," said the bartender.

"Another drink—yes—but not to forget."

Brick spent about an hour in the store. He bought a dark suit, shirts, boots, hat, and a cartridge belt and holster. The belt and holster were second hand, and fitted well. In a little saddle store next door he got a pair of second-hand bat-wing chaps and a pair of spurs. The saddle maker let him change clothes in the back room, and he came out of there looking like the old Brick Davidson of Sun Dog, except that he needed a shave and a haircut.

A few doors farther down the street was a barber shop, and when Brick came out of there, smelling of hair tonic and witch hazel, he was fit to face the world or anybody in it. As he walked up the street, two men rode in and tied their horses. Brick saw the sunlight flash on a badge pinned to a shirt front, and he wondered if this man had ever been called upon to hang a friend. They were standing in front of the store as he came up, and nodded pleasantly.

"Howdy, gents," smiled Brick. "Nice weather we're having."

The sheriff smiled. "Not bad, is it? I don't believe I ever met you?"

"I know danged well yuh never have—at least, not down here. I just got in a while ago. My name's Davidson."

"My name's Campbell, Davidson. Shake hands with Ortego; he's my deputy."

"Pleased to meetcha," grinned Brick. "How's crime down here?"

"About like it is every other place, I reckon," said the sheriff. "Are you from the North?"

"Yeah. Not enough to be an Eskimo, but enough to freeze my ears in the winter."

They laughed with Brick. Campbell said he had spent several winters in Alberta, and that he was perfectly willing to stay where no snow fell. As they were talking, Joe Pico and the dealer came from the cantina and stopped near the sorrel horse. Pico seemed rather drunk.

"They're admirin' my horse," grinned Brick.

"Is that yore sorrel?" asked the sheriff.

Brick nodded. "I won him a while ago. That tall jigger over there thought he could play stud."

"That's Joe Pico," said Ortego; and added, "From Gomez Springs."

Brick squinted thoughtfully.

"Is Gomez Springs near here?"

"Down across the Border—about six miles from here."

"What kind of a place is it?"

"Not so good for a gringo."

"Gringo is a white man, ain't it? What have they got against us?"

"Mexico for Mexicans," said the sheriff dryly.

"Didja ever know anybody by the name of Jim Breen around here?"

"He lives in Gomez Springs," said Ortego. "I know him."

Brick was interested.

"What is his business?"

Ortego shrugged his shoulders. "Quien sabe? He comes here once in a while, and seems to have plenty money."

"Didja ever know a feller named Scotty McKee?"

"Sure," nodded the sheriff. "Scotty used to own the One Oak Cantina over there. Sold out to Ed Pico, I think. I dunno where Scotty went from here."

Brick was learning things fast. Until he heard Gomez Springs mentioned, he had no idea he was in the country where Scotty McKee used to live.

"How do I get out to that Rose ranch?" he asked.

"The Rancho del Rosa? Take the road straight east of here, and yuh can't miss it."

"I heard they might need another puncher."

"I don't know about that," said the sheriff. "Bob Maxwell usually has quite a crew."

"Lots of cattle?"

"Quite a few, I reckon."

Brick thanked them and started across the street. The dealer had gone back in the cantina, but Joe Pico lounged in the doorway, smoking a cigarette. Brick walked over and untied the sorrel, talking softly to the animal. Pico lurched away from the doorway and came out toward Brick, his swarthy face twisted in a scowl.

"What you going to do weeth my horse?" he asked.

Brick turned his head, a puzzled frown between his blue eyes. "Yore horse?"

"My horse—of course."

Brick turned and rested his hands on his hips.

"Is yore memory so short that yuh don't remember losin' him?"

"You have a bill of sale from me?"

"No, I never got one. But I won this horse, and I take him now."

"You think twice, my friend. You have nothing to show ownership."

"What kind of a skin game is this?" demanded Brick hotly.

"Not any skin game," smiled Pico. "The horse is mine."

"Yo're cock-eyed and crazy!" snorted Brick. "Just watch and see if I don't take this horse."

Brick turned and looped the rope around the saddle horn.

"Jus' a moment," said Pico softly.

Brick jerked around, facing Pico, who had half-drawn his gun.

"We do not wait for the law to deal with horse-thieves down here," said Pico meaningly.

It was a foolish move on Pico's part, unless he intended to carry it through. Perhaps he had an idea that the half-drawn gun would intimidate the red-headed cowboy. At any rate, Pico was totally unprepared for what followed. Brick's right hand snapped down to his holster, jerked up with the same movement, and Joe Pico went staggering back and sideways, when Brick's heavy bullet smashed through his right shoulder.

Pico's gun thudded into the dirt and Pico stopped, sitting down against the wall of the cantina, a very surprised and foolish expression in his face. Brick didn't move for several moments. The sheriff and deputy were coming across the street. They had seen everything, but did not hear what had been said. The bartender, dealer, and a couple of customers crowded the cantina doorway, and men were coming from all points of the compass.

"What seemed to be the trouble?" asked the sheriff.

Brick stepped past him and faced the men in the doorway.

"Any of you fellers want to tell the world that I didn't win that horse and saddle?" he asked coldly.

"You won it," said the dealer quickly. "Joe was drunk."

Brick turned to the sheriff. "He tried to tell me that I didn't own that horse and saddle. Accused me of tryin' to steal it."

"It's all right," said the sheriff. "I seen Pico draw his gun, and you got him quick. Some of you fellers better get a doctor. The horse belongs to you, Davidson."

"Thank yuh, Sheriff."

Brick walked over to the horse and started to mount, when the sheriff came in close to him.

"Watch out for the Pico gang," he warned Brick.

"There's several of 'em, and this is the first time that one of 'em has been downed."

"Thank yuh kindly," smiled Brick, and swung into the saddle.

He thrilled at the feel of a good horse between his knees, the fit of a well-made saddle. It was the first time he had been on a horse since he had left Sun Dog. He had ridden into Sicomoro on the rickety wagon of a Mexican wood peddler, dirty, ragged, and with only a dollar to his name. Two hours later he was riding away, well-dressed, clean-shaven, with money in his pocket, astride his own horse and sitting in a silver-trimmed saddle.

"And still they try to tell us that it's wrong to gamble," he said whimsically. "When the goddess of luck smiles on yuh, yo're a fool if yuh don't make a fuss over her. Now, all I've got to do is get me a job and look out for the Pico family; and the job worries me the most."

He rode along for a little way, examining the silver trimming on the fork of the saddle. Finally he stopped, took out his heavy-bladed pocket-knife and proceeded to pry loose the silver rivets. It was a simple matter to strip off all the silver, which was really only a silver plating on white metal. The saddle was so nearly new that there was little indication that the leather had ever been covered.

Brick threw the silver aside as though it were worthless, and rode on.

"I'd look well, huntin' for a job in a saddle like this one was," he told himself. "I'd look like a mail-order puncher, makin' a flash."

He traveled along the narrow, dusty road, through the boulder-strewn hills, the leavings of the ice age, when a tired glacier stopped to melt in a strange sun. Around and among the boulders grew thorny mesquite, creosote bushes, sage, cactus, and an occasional desert smoke-tree, looking at a distance like a puff of yellow smoke.

A sidewinder, the little desert rattlesnake, crossed the road ahead of Brick, and he drew rein to watch the little fellow angle its way into the weeds beside the road. A sage rabbit hopped softly into the road, saw the horse only a few feet away, and seemed to fairly explode in a cloud of dust.

Brick lounged sideways in his saddle, scanning the country to the south. Those mountains down there were in an alien land. Brick wondered where Silent Slade had gone. He and Brick had often talked about the address on that letter and the few crumbs of marahuana weed in the old tobacco sack.

Brick felt sure that Silent would go as far as his hundred dollars would take him. Silent would never go East; the West coast would hardly be far enough away from Sun Dog, because when Sun Dog County broadcasted his description, it would be difficult for a cowboy of Silent's stature to escape detection. His best chance would be in the Southwest, where in a case of necessity he could step over into Mexico.

As Brick rode along his eye caught the flash of a bit of color which did not seem a part of the natural hues of nature. It was a vermilion flash in the sunlight. Brick drew up his horse for a moment, and then swung off the road. The brush was scarcely knee-high here, with bare patches of alkali. About fifty yards from the road he found the patch of vermilion.

It was the handkerchief around the neck of a dead cowboy. He was lying flat on his back, arms outspread, one hand still clutching a blue Colt revolver. The man was of medium height, blond, with a deep scar across his left cheek and the side of his nose. He was dressed in a gray shirt, overalls, and boots. His hat, a black Stetson with a silver trimmed band, was lying against a bush several feet away. Brick could see where the blood had oozed from a bullet wound just above the left pocket of his gray shirt. Brick didn't need to examine him, nor did he dismount. It was a job for the sheriff.

Brick rode back, tied his handkerchief to a bush on the left side of the road to mark the spot, and rode on. It was less than a mile to the Rancho del Rosa. The road led straight in through one of the wide arches of the patio, and the sorrel stopped at the water tub beside the well.

Brick relaxed and looked around. He had never seen anything like this old patio, the old adobe walls of the buildings, half-covered with roses and ivy. Suddenly he realized that he was looking at a girl, who had been seated on a bench in the shade of the roses, but was coming toward him now. He dismounted quickly and removed his hat.

"I beg yore pardon, Ma'am," he smiled. "I was so kinda taken up by this place that I plumb forgot it might belong to somebody."

"Hablar Español?" she asked, smiling at him.

"That's the worst of it," complained Brick. "I can say buenas dias and buenas noches, but that don't make much conversation."

"Then I'll talk English."

"That's my tongue," laughed Brick. "Mebby I'll learn the other, but I'd hate to miss talkin' to yuh, while I'm learnin'. Ma'am, I'm Arthur William Davidson, but on account of my auburn hair, they call me Brick. And I'm lookin' for a man named Maxwell. Bob Maxwell, I think."

"That's my father. I am Marie Maxwell."

"Well, I'm shore glad to meetcha, Miss Maxwell. Nice place yuh got here."

"I love it," she said simply.

"Then that makes me and you jist even—so do I."

They were smiling at each other, when a man came from the bunk-house. He was a short,

50

heavily built man, evidently a Mexican. His hair was rather long, and a heavy, black mustache covered his upper lip.

"Leo, will you please tell Mr. Maxwell that a man wishes to see him?" said Marie.

"Si, Señorita," the man smiled pleasantly, and went into the house.

A few moments later Bob Maxwell came out. He was a big, lean-faced man, rather swarthy, dark-eyed, his black hair turning gray in spots. He smiled at his daughter, who introduced him to Brick.

"I jist kinda rode in on yuh," grinned Brick. "I'm lookin' for a job, Mr. Maxwell."

"A job, eh?" Maxwell looked keenly at Brick. "What kind of a job?"

"Punchin' cows."

"Oh, yes."

"I was jist driftin' through," said Brick earnestly, "and I heard that you handle quite a lot of cows down here. I needed a job pretty bad; so I came along lookin' for one."

"I see. Well, I'm sorry, Davidson; but just at present I have enough men."

"That makes it tough, don't it? Do you know any other ranch that might need a man?"

"No, I don't."

"Uh-huh," thoughtfully. "Say, I almost forgot. About a mile back toward that town of Sicomoro, on the south side of the road, you'll find a dead

51

man. I hung my handkerchief on a bush beside the road, to mark the place."

"A—a dead man?" faltered Maxwell.

"Shore. Somebody spotted him a dead-center shot. I got a flash of red out there, and I—"

"You say the man has been shot?"

"Shore. I dunno how long he's—"

"What does he look like?" interrupted Maxwell.

"Oh, he's about my size, I reckon. Kinda blond, and he's got a scar on one cheek and on his nose."

The blood seemed to drain from Maxwell's face, as he and Marie exchanged glances.

"Dell Harper!" exclaimed Marie.

"You say he was shot?" asked Maxwell blankly.

"Well, I didn't probe for no bullet, if that's what yuh mean. He's dead, and he's got a gun in one hand. Mebby he shot himself. But there didn't seem to be any burns on his shirt. I jist looked at him and came on."

Maxwell rubbed his hands together nervously, started for the bunk-house, but turned and went back to the veranda, where he called to the man whom Marie had addressed as Leo. They exchanged a few words in Spanish, and Leo went running across the patio, going out through the rear arch, toward the stables.

Maxwell came back to Marie and Brick.

"The dead man was my foreman," he told Brick.

"That's too bad. I saw the sheriff in Sicomoro just before I left."

Maxwell muttered something under his breath and walked out toward the stables, where Leo Herrera was saddling two horses.

"That's kinda tough luck," said Brick slowly. "Has he been with yuh long, Miss Maxwell?"

"He has been with the rancho a long time, Mr. Davidson. I have only been here less than a year, except when I was a little girl. You see, I have been away to school mostly all my life."

Brick's mind flashed back to Juanita McKee.

"I don't see who could have killed Dell Harper," she said. "He seemed very nice. But some one is always getting shot down here, it seems to me. There is always trouble along the Border."

"I've heard there was," replied Brick. "I reckon the Mexicans make things kinda lively, don't they?"

Marie did not reply. Her father and Herrera were coming in with their horses.

"You say you marked the spot with a handkerchief, Davidson?" asked Maxwell.

"Sure—on the south side of the road. I'll go back with yuh, if yuh—"

"That isn't necessary," quickly. "You might put up your horse and stay here a while—at least, for the day. I—I might be able to use you."

"That would be fine," grinned Brick.

53

"You'll find the stable out that entrance. Plenty of empty stalls."

Brick thanked him, nodded to Marie, and led his horse back to the stable, where he unsaddled the animal and gave it a feed of oats. He came back to the patio and sat down on a bench in the shade to smoke a cigarette. It had been a hard day for Brick, and he was a little weary.

After a few puffs on his cigarette he stretched out on the bench, pillowed his head on his arms, and went to sleep under the bower of climbing roses. But Brick was a light sleeper, and the sound of horses walking across the patio awakened him. He turned his head sideways and saw two riders near the old well.

One was a big man, wearing a huge Mexican sombrero, while the other was of medium height, slender, and, as Brick expressed it, all dogged out fit for a scandal. His blue silk shirt was ornamented with huge pearl buttons, his black trousers fit like the skin on a sausage, and on his feet he wore high-heeled patent-leather boots. His sombrero was nearly white, surmounted with a black, silver-studded band, his neckerchief was scarlet, and around his slim waist was a fancy sash, beneath his silver-studded cartridge belt.

"If that jigger busts into song, I'll know I'm at a show," mused Brick, now wide awake. "Golly, ain't he a shiner!"

The big man did not dismount, and kept his back to Brick. Neither of them had seen him on the bench. They talked for several moments, and then the slender man adjusted his sash and walked over to the steps of the veranda, as Marie came out. At sight of him she stopped short. From her actions, it was evident that either they were strangers to each other, or Marie didn't like him.

Brick couldn't hear what was said, but he heard the man laugh, and say something in Spanish. Marie came out to the steps, and, although Brick could not understand Spanish, it was evident that she was telling him that she did not care to talk further with him.

But the man persisted. He became eloquent with his hands. Marie turned to go back in the house, but he grasped her by the wrist and drew her back. She tried to jerk away, but he tightened his grip.

"What she's tellin' him now would burn a hole in the ice," said Brick to himself.

He uncoiled from the bench, took several steps toward the porch, hooking his thumbs over the top of his belt.

"You better let loose of the lady," he said clearly.

The man whirled quickly, glaring at Brick. The big man turned in his saddle, disclosing a huge black beard, which grew out from his face like the bristles on a hair-brush. Brick was not grinning now, and his mop of red hair was like burnished copper in the sunlight.

The man released Marie, who stepped back quickly.

"And who are you?" asked the dandy coldly.

"I'm the whippoorwill that made you behave yourself."

"And what is this affair to you?"

"Start somethin', and you'll find out," said Brick.

The man looked at Marie and back at Brick, who was slowly balancing himself on the balls of his feet. His fingers were splayed out a little, but the thumb was still resting on the top edge of his belt. It was a danger signal, and the man read it rightly. With a shrug of indifference he turned, bowed gracefully to Marie, came slowly down the steps and walked out to his horse, ignoring Brick entirely.

But Brick did not take his eyes off the man, who swung gracefully into the saddle. He swung his horse around to the left, presenting his back to Brick, but for several moments the big man continued to look at Brick, who was staring at him now, his jaw sagging a little. Then the big man turned his horse around and followed the other, but, as they rode out through the east archway, the big man gave a backward wave of his left hand, but did not lift it above his knee.

Brick relaxed slowly. Marie had come to the edge of the porch and was looking at him.

"Thank you," she said.

"Thasall right, Ma'am. He ain't exactly an old friend of the family, is he?"

"He is an old friend of my father."

"Oh, yeah."

"His name is Jim Breen."

"Well, can yuh imagine that? Jim Breen, eh?"

"You knew him?"

Brick took a deep breath and shook his head.

"No, Ma'am, I never seen him before; but I've heard the name. Do yuh know the man who was with him?"

"No, I don't believe I have ever seen him before. Jim Breen came to see my father."

"I suppose that's why he pawed you around thataway. He'll probably tell yore dad about me, and I won't have no more job than a jack rabbit. Still, I don't suppose yore dad wants to have folks pawin' you around."

"Well, I don't, at least, Mr. Davidson—and I thank you again."

"Neither do I—and yo're welcome," grinned Brick.

Marie started to walk back into the house, but came out again.

"I'm sorry it happened," she told Brick. "Jim Breen and my father are close friends, and I—I hope he will understand."

"Jim Breen?"

"No, my father."

"Don't let that worry yuh none," grinned Brick.

"But you wanted to work here, and—"

"Shucks!" laughed Brick. "Why, I ain't got the job yet. Prob'ly never will; so don't let that worry yuh. I'm sorry it happened, Ma'am; but when yuh stop to consider that it could have been a lot worse."

"I was afraid it would be, Mr. Davidson. Jim Breen is rather an impulsive person."

"I noticed that. Still, he never got impulsive with me."

Marie smiled and walked away, while Brick went back to the bench in the shade of the roses, where he rolled a cigarette. His fingers trembled just a little, but it was not the reaction from his near encounter with Jim Breen—it was because he recognized the bearded man as Silent Slade.

"Can yuh beat that?" Brick asked himself. "Silent trailin' with Jim Breen! What kind of a mess is this down here, anyway? I have to shoot a man to collect the horse I won fairly, then I find a dead man, sprawled in the sun, a bullet through his heart. And then to find Silent with the man whose name was on that envelope.

"A friend of Maxwell, is he? And he tries to paw Maxwell's daughter, who is scared that my interference might cause complications. I've been in this country half a day, and I've made plenty enemies. That's what yuh git for havin' red hair, I s'pose. Hm-m-m. If I was showin' any sense, I'd saddle my bronc and keep on goin'. Silent didn't want to know me, but he slipped me a signal; so I reckon I'll stick around and see what the big feller has on his mind."

It was about two hours later when Maxwell came back. Herrera was not with him, but he was accompanied by Campbell, the sheriff, and another man. This other man was rather tall, slender, hardfaced, his skin burned to the texture of leather.

Brick noticed that Maxwell seemed greatly depressed and tired. He immediately went into the house. The sheriff introduced Brick to the stranger, whose name was Berry.

"Mr. Berry is one of the Border Patrol," explained the sheriff.

"I've heard about you folks," smiled Brick.

"Nothin' good, I'll bet," said Berry.

"All accordin' to who tells it. How was the patient gettin' along when you left, Sheriff?"

"Pico? Oh, he'll get well. Damn fools are hard to kill, Davidson. Maxwell tells me that you were the one who found Harper, the dead man, out there along the road."

Brick explained how he happened to see the flash of color, and found the dead man.

"I didn't know who he was until I described him to Maxwell. Who do yuh think killed him?"

The sheriff shook his head slowly. "No idea, Davidson."

"You're a stranger down here, ain't yuh?" asked Berry.

"Yeah, but I seem to be gettin' acquainted in a hurry," laughed Brick.

"But not enough to understand local conditions. You're from the North?"

"Montana."

"I see. Are you goin' to work for Maxwell?"

"That's a question. I haven't been hired yet."

"Maxwell is a fine man, Davidson. The killin' of his foreman has hit him mighty hard. Harper has been with him a long time. There's quite a lot of killin' done along this part of the Border, but we can account for quite a lot of it, because of the constant feud between the smugglers and the hijackers."

"The hijacker is the feller who steals from the smuggler, ain't he?"

"That's the idea," smiled Berry. "As soon as the smuggler has done all the dangerous work, the hijacker takes the stuff away from him."

"Can yuh blame the smuggler for killin' him?" asked Brick.

"Well," smiled Berry, "from the smuggler's viewpoint, it's justifiable homicide, I suppose. But it all goes to make things hard for us."

"Yuh don't mean that this Harper was mixed up with one faction or the other, do yuh?"

The officer shook his head quickly. "There has never been any suspicion about Harper or anybody connected with the Rancho del Rosa."

"You asked about Jim Breen," reminded the sheriff. "He was in town when we left there."

"Do you know Jim Breen?" asked Berry.

"Never met him. I jist heard about him, thasall."

The two officers shook hands with Brick, and rode away. A few minutes later, Maxwell came out and Brick crossed the patio to him. Maxwell looked Brick over, a troubled expression in his eyes.

"I'm sorry about what happened a while ago, Davidson," he said slowly. "I'm sure Jim Breen didn't—he's of rather an impulsivc nature, you see. Marie told me. I heard what happened between you and Joe Pico. That was rather unfortunate. Now, I'm putting it up to you, whether you stay or not."

"You mean that I get the job, unless I'm scared to stay here?"

"That's the situation exactly."

"I'll stay."

Maxwell smiled thinly. "That's what Marie said."

"I guess it's my red hair," grinned Brick.

CHAPTER III

BRICK HORNS IN ON A CONFERENCE

IN the days that followed, Brick learned much of the local history. There were only five cowboys, including Brick, employed at the Rancho del Rosa; "Slim" Neeley, a long-geared cowboy from the Panhandle; Buck Eads, a hard-headed waddy from New Mexico; Leo Herrera; and Johnny Snow, younger than the rest, a wild-riding young man from eastern Oregon.

Brick liked Johnny the best of the lot, and it didn't take Brick long to discover that the youngster was in love with Marie. He admitted frankly that Marie didn't know it.

"Ain't she a pippin, Brick?" he asked, as they rode the brushy hills north of Sicomoro. "She's just fine. But, boy, I've got my work cut out. Her old man wants her to marry Jim Breen. Can yuh imagine that? No, yuh can't because yuh don't know Breen."

None of the boys knew of the incident which had happened in the patio the day Brick arrived at the rancho.

"But does she want to marry Jim Breen?" asked Brick.

"Quien sabe? She's half-Spanish or Mexican, and she *might* do what her old man tells her to do. Ed Pico used to ramble down here to see her once in a while, but Maxwell shore stopped that in a hurry. I wish I'd been in Sicomoro the day you pasted a hunk of lead into Joe Pico. He's mucho malo, that hombre. And you want to look a little out, Brick. Ed Pico ain't so liable to mix into it, but there's Dave, Joe's brother, and Al Abelardo and Bill Abelardo, Joe's cousins. They're bad. Wish I knew who killed Dell Harper."

"Did you ever know a feller named Scotty McKee?"

"Sho-o-ore! He used to run the Solo Encinas Cantina in Sicomoro. He was all right, too. But all of a sudden he sold out to Ed Pico, and faded out of the country. That was over a year ago."

"What does Jim Breen do for a livin'?"

"Oh, he's half owner of the big cantina and gamblin' house in Gomez Wells, and he's got a little rancho about a mile below the Border, kinda southeast of Sicomoro. Wait'll yuh see him, Brick. He's the fanciest dresser you ever seen. He's got one vest with turquoise buttons. It's a fact. And he's plenty rapido with a six-gun."

"Got plenty nerve?"

"Well," grinned Johnny, "it takes nerve to dress the way he does."

"I suppose the Border Patrol has a job to handle down here."

"Shore. But what can they do? They don't get much help from anybody, because it's dangerous to buck either element. Me, I'm just a waddy, gettin' along. There's a lot of money to be made down here, if yuh want to take a chance on the hot end of a bullet or the inside of a Federal penitentiary. I don't, I'm plenty sure."

"Nor me," grinned Brick. "I was just wonderin' which side of the fence Jim Breen would be on—if any."

"Well, he wouldn't hardly be a hijacker, Brick. He'd last about as long as a snowball in hell. You can bet yore last pair of socks that anybody livin' in Mejico is either a smuggler or nothin'. Gomez Springs is only about five hundred inhabitants, but it draws from a lotta country. Old Miguel Gomez used to own the town, until Diaz came along and cut him off at the pockets. He nailed the old man, but he missed the son, who is worse than the old man ever was. Lobo Gomez don't own the town, of course, but he thinks he does.

"He's a great big ignorant greaser, part Injun, with an inflated idea of what he is. He don't dare cross the border, because he's pulled enough rough stuff to draw a first-class bullet. I've heard that Lobo is the sweet young thing who brings the contraband to Gomez Springs for the lusty smugglers. He gets his percentage, without any danger, except from his own Government, which recognizes him as a dirty deuce in their dog-eared pack of outlaws, and not of enough importance to bother about killin'."

"We'll have to go down to Gomez Springs some day," smiled Brick.

"I'll go," grinned Johnny. "The last time I was down there, me and Slim Neeley shore came away in a hurry. A fat-headed gringo got into some kinda trouble in the big cantina, and me and Slim elects to help him out. Yuh can't allow yore own kind to get the worst of it in a foreign land, can yuh?

"I dunno, what the total loss was, but my gun was empty when we piled this gringo on a horse in front of Slim and headed north. He had been hit over the head kinda hard, and Slim had a job holdin' him upright. Anyway, we beat the gang to the border and took the feller to Sicomoro, where we set him down on a sidewalk in the light from a window. He's plumb conscious now, but he's got an egg-sized lump on his head. He looks up at Slim and says: 'Deutschland uber alles.'

"And me and Slim ain't been down there since. Slim ain't got no sense of humor, anyway. He says that next time he's goin' to know more about a man before he horns in on a rescue party."

"What do yuh think of the Mexicans as a people?" asked Brick.

"Fine. The real honest-to-gosh Mexican is fine. They're honest and proud as the devil. We don't get many of 'em up here. You can't no more judge the Mexican people by what yuh find along here than yuh can judge the white races by these Border toughs. Most any old time yuh find a tough gang of Mexicans, you'll find a white man leadin' 'em."

"Breen is an American, ain't he?"

"From Indiana," laughed Johnny. "He's a fair sample. I'm wonderin' why yo're so interested in Breen, when yuh say yuh don't know him."

"I reckon I did kinda speak about him often," smiled Brick. "But I've got a reason, pardner. I'll let yuh in on somethin', if you'll keep it under yore hat."

And while they rode back to the rancho, Brick told Johnny Snow the story of what had happened in Sun Dog. Johnny was rather amazed over it all, and more so, when Brick told him what had happened that day at the Ranch of the Roses.

"And this big feller was yore old bunkie, eh?" he marveled. "Ridin' with Jim Breen! Can yuh imagine that? Shore sounds like one of them story books, this idea of you comin' all the way down here, and all this happenin'. And he recognized yuh? Say, that must have been a shock."

"It was a shock," grinned Brick. "I didn't even know he was headin' for this country, but I kinda had a hunch."

"Well," said Johnny seriously, "I don't like Breen and I ain't got no use for the Pico outfit; so if yuh don't mind, I'd like to set in with yuh on this game. No, I ain't got nobody to mourn my loss. I was an orphan further back than I remember; so there's nobody, except the sheriff, to notify in case I get stopped short."

"That's shore nice of yuh, pardner; but I ain't askin' for help."

"I'm just offerin' it, Brick."

"Thank yuh, Johnny," seriously. "I'm hopin' for peace."

"So am I, but I'll keep on wearin' a gun."

It was hard for Brick to connect the Rancho del Rosa with trouble and strife. It seemed so peaceful there. An old Mexican woman, whom the boys called Mujer, served their meals out on the veranda which overlooked the patio. The work was light at this time of the year. The inquest over the body of Dell Harper was a mere formality, in which Brick was obliged to testify concerning the discovery of the body.

They buried him in the little cemetery at Sicomoro, and another Border mystery was in a fair way never to be solved. Brick saw Ed Pico and the Abelardo brothers at the funeral, but they paid no attention to him. Joe Pico was getting along well, according to the sheriff, who talked with Brick after the funeral. Berry and another of the Border Patrol were at the funeral, and Brick saw Berry point him out to the other officer.

After the funeral service, Berry shook hands with Brick and introduced him to Mitchell, the other officer.

Brick had had little chance to talk with Bob Maxwell since that first day. Maxwell had appointed Slim Neeley foreman, and the boys took their orders from Slim. But Brick had an idea that something was bothering Maxwell. He seemed nervous, irritable, inclined to keep to himself.

Brick mentioned it to Johnny Snow.

"I didn't think anythin' about it until yuh mentioned it," said Johnny. "There *is* a change in the old man."

Maxwell was by no means an old man, but most of the boys referred to him by that title.

"Mebby he's worryin' about Harper bein' killed," suggested Brick.

"That might be. He's got somethin' on his mind. It might be Jim Breen. You say Marie told him about Breen grabbin' her by the wrist. Mebby it bothers him."

"What would prevent a gang from across the Border rustlin' Maxwell's cattle?"

"Nothin'. That's been done a-plenty, but not just around here. Maxwell has always minded his own business, been friends with everybody, and his cattle have been left alone. I think that's why

68

he's minded his own business all this time. Bob Maxwell is nobody's fool, Brick."

"No, I reckon not; but I hope he don't marry his daughter off to a damn renegade like Breen, who ain't neither white nor Mexican."

"If Breen knew what I think about it, he'd shoot me in the dark of the moon," said Johnny seriously.

That evening Buck Eads was dealing écarté in the bunk-house and the boys were playing two-bit stakes, except Johnny, who was out at the stable. He had snapped his rope in the middle that afternoon, and was putting a hondo on a new one.

It was about nine o'clock when Johnny came in. He managed to catch Brick's eye, and flashed him a signal to come outside. Brick yawned and sauntered outside, where he found Johnny.

"Jim Breen came in about five minutes ago," whispered Johnny. "He was all alone. I think that him and the old man are up there in that corner room, where yuh see the light. I hate like hell to listen in on anybody, but we could use that long ladder—and I don't think the window is all the way down."

"I'm shore surprised at you," said Brick earnestly. "Where's the ladder?"

Together they secured the ladder, which reached to the upper balcony, leaning it softly against the old railing.

"I'll do the listenin'," whispered Brick. "If they catch me, it'll be all right. You don't want to lose yore job, yuh know."

Johnny made no comments, but stood at the foot of the ladder in the deep shadow, while Brick climbed silently to the balcony, and crossed over to the window. The curtains were closed, but the voices of the two men were audible. Maxwell was talking angrily.

". . . always been square, Jim, and you know it. If Dell had them, which I doubt, he'd—"

"Wait a minute, Bob," said Breen. "That remark reflects back on me. I tell you he had 'em. Wong Kee sent 'em across by Dell. He told me he did, and Wong Kee never lied to us in his life. We've always trusted him, because he had more brains than any of us. It was his job to scheme out things to beat the customs and the hijackers, and you know how well he's done it. If Wong Kee says he sent 'em across by Dell Harper, that's what he done, Bob. Wong Kee was as honest as a dollar."

"Why do you say 'was'?"

"Because," said Breen slowly, "Wong Kee got into a mess with several other Chinks in a fan-tan game that night, and died with a knife between his shoulders."

"My God! Do you mean to tell me that nobody knows how they were sent?"

"You know well enough that Wong Kee never

told anybody, except the man he selected to take the stuff across. He wouldn't work any other way."

"And both of them are dead! Jim, don't you realize what it means? Every cent I'm worth is gone. Oh, I've been afraid of something like this all the time. Trusting a damn Chinaman!"

"But who got 'em?" demanded Breen. "Who killed Harper? The hijackers never got 'em. They knew that the stuff was coming across. Don't ask me how they found out. There always is leaks."

"Leaks!" groaned Maxwell. "And I mortgaged everything I owned to put this deal over. Well, I'm down and out."

"Are you?" Breen did not seem convinced. "I had a lot of money in the deal, and so did others. They don't know you as well as I do."

"You don't mean to say they think *I* got 'em?"

"I didn't think so, Bob. They've been investigating, but they're fully convinced that the hijackers didn't get 'em. It's a cinch that the Border Patrol didn't, or they'd be crowing loud enough to be heard back in Washington. Now, what's to be done?"

"Oh, I don't know."

"You better come over the line and convince the others that you didn't double-cross anybody."

"I'll do nothing of the kind."

"Suit yourself. I'll go back and tell them that you deny having anything to do with it. I lose ten

71

thousand dollars, but that's all right; I'm not whining."

"Suppose Wong Kee never sent 'em across? Suppose somebody knifed him for the layout, Jim?"

"Not a chance. We've investigated that, too. What became of that damn red-headed puncher who got smart with me the other day? I suppose you heard about it."

"I heard about it and gave him a job."

"Oh, yuh did, eh? On the strength of the deal, I suppose."

"Breen, we better come to an understanding. Marie don't like you. She has told me that a number of times. She's old enough to know what she wants. Leave her alone from now on."

Breen laughed shortly.

"Oh, well," he said, "I suppose I did get a little rough. But she got mad at me and told me a few things I didn't care to hear. But I don't intend to let that redhead get away with any tough stuff."

"He's the one who put Joe Pico in care of the doctor."

"That was fine! I wish he'd lead up the whole Pico outfit; but he better not make any more breaks toward me. I'm goin' back now, and I'll try to explain to the boys."

"I don't think any explanation is needed. If they can find out who killed Harper, they'll find the stuff. I'm sure I didn't kill him."

"Well, I'll talk to 'em, Bob."

As they left the room, Brick hurried down the ladder. Swiftly they put it away and were out at the stable when Breen came out alone and rode away. Brick didn't know how much he ought to tell Johnny, but finally decided to keep most of it to himself.

"It was about Marie," he told Johnny. "Breen was sore about what happened here the other day. I reckon he's out to get me. Anyway, Maxwell told him to leave Marie alone from now on."

"Gee, that's great! What did Breen say?"

"He didn't like it, but he didn't complain."

"Maxwell better not trust him too far."

"I'll betcha Maxwell knows it."

"I don't see how Maxwell can afford to mix with Breen. If the Border officers—but they all know the old man is on the square. Brick, I'm sure glad I thought of that ladder. Let's go and see if we can't clean up Buck's écarté game."

Brick played a few more hands of écarté, but finally went to bed. He wanted a chance to think things over. He knew now that Maxwell was a smuggler, in cahoots with Jim Breen. It was evident that a valuable cargo had gone astray, and it had to do with the killing of Dell Harper. He had heard Maxwell declare that he had mortgaged the rancho in order to put over the deal, and that this would break him.

No wonder Maxwell had seemed nervous.

Brick wondered what kind of a cargo it was; a cargo small enough for one man to carry, and still be of such value. From the conversation Brick had overheard, he surmised that a Chinaman named Wong Kee was the one who figured out the ways to send the stuff across.

Brick realized that it would require a keen mind to devise ways of outwitting the Border Patrol and the hijackers, and that a Chinaman might well be mentally equipped to handle this kind of a job. Wong Kee had evidently sent the stuff across the line by Harper, and then got himself killed in a fan-tan game, without disclosing to Jim Breen the method used in that particular case. With both Harper and Wong Kee dead, no man knew how it had been sent.

Brick knew nothing of the smuggling game, except that they were a desperate lot of men, who apparently stopped at nothing to complete their work. If Jim Breen was a smuggler, which he apparently was, Silent Slade was working at the same game. When Johnny crawled into the bunk beside Brick, the redhead whispered to him:

"How many drugs could one man carry?"

"Kinds or value?" grinned Johnny.

"Value."

"Oh, I dunno, Brick; a good many thousands of dollars' worth, I reckon. You wasn't thinkin' of packin' in a supply, was yuh?"

"No, I was just wonderin' about it."

"Well, it's a bum job. I don't mind what else they smuggle in, but I'm shore against dope. Know anythin' about drugs?"

"Not much, Johnny. What's marahuana?"

"The worst loco weed on earth. Grows down here, and the Mexicans smoke it in with their tobacco. Oh, it shore freezes their nerves all right. Too mucho, and they go hay-wire—crazy. And it shore hits a white man hard."

"Do white men use it?"

"Do they? Show me anythin' a white man won't do. We're a versatile race, cowboy. Say, do yuh reckon the old man was serious when he told Jim Breen to keep away from Marie? I don't blame the old man for tellin' that jigger to keep away from the girl; but the old man better not get in bad with Breen. I figure Breen is a grande hombre down across the line, and he could shore deal this rancho a plenty trouble.

"Me, I'd jist as soon swap lead with that bunch as not. I've got jist a faint suspicion that a lot of them lazy jiggers has been fattenin' their insides with Maxwell cattle for a long time, and if any trouble ever busts, they'll clean out the Rancho del Rosa pretty pronto. A man couldn't run fast enough to give me a ranch this near the Border."

"Won't the Mexican Government give us any protection?"

"How can they? They used to have a bunch of soldados over at Gomez Springs, but they moved 'em out. Yore protection is to stay on this side of the line, pardner."

"Well," said Brick sleepily, "I dunno whether I want to go over there or not."

"Aw, it's fun," laughed Johnny. "I suppose they're layin' for me and Slim. He won't go. He says, what's the use? Kill off a dozen contra-bandistas to rescue a Dutchman. Slim's practical. We'll go over and see what she looks like. I missed one jigger twice, and he might hold still the next time. Ho-hum-m-m-m. Good-night."

CHAPTER IV

SILENT SLADE, OUTLAW

SILENT SLADE didn't know yet what it was all about. After he left Marlin City, he rode as far as the hundred dollars would take him, and then kept right on going South. He had a vague idea of going straight through to Central or South America. He rode on freight trains, asked for rides along the highways, and when there wasn't anything better, he walked. An occasional job provided him with food, but he did not stop long in any one place.

He realized that the law had a long arm. His whiskers and hair grew long, but his great size was undisguisable. He came to Sicomoro much in the same way as Brick Davidson did a little later, found a sheriff there and kept right on down across the line, ending his pilgrimage at Gomez Springs. The name of Jim Breen was vaguely familiar, but he did not connect it with the name Brick had found on that letter.

It didn't take Silent long to discover that Gomez Springs was sort of a haven for "wanted" men. Breen gave him a job in the big cantina, as sort of a "bouncer," but was obliged to take him off the job because Silent did not understand Spanish. Breen had four renegade whites,

77

Mahan, Eddy, Kelsey, and Berg, taking care of his rancho; so he sent Silent with them. Together with a buck-tooth Chinaman, Ling, they made up the personnel of Breen's rancho, where one man could have handled the work.

Silent didn't like the outfit, and it took him quite a while to resign himself to their companionship. Berg told Silent that Mahan had killed a policeman in Yuma, Kelsey was wanted for a mail robbery and a killing, and Eddy was wanted for things too numerous to mention. Berg didn't say what he was wanted for, but Kelsey told Silent that Berg didn't dare poke his nose across the line.

Silent drank too much tequila one day, and confided to Kelsey that he was under sentence to hang for a murder in Montana. This information gave Silent a good standing on the rancho and in Gomez Springs. It just happened that Breen asked Silent to ride with him the day they went to the Rancho del Rosa. Silent had no liking for that side of the line, but he went along, and he was rather in a daze for several hours after seeing Brick Davidson in the patio of the rancho. He wanted to stay and join forces with Brick, but his better judgment told him to go back.

Breen was angry over Brick's interference, but said nothing to Silent. Silent told the boys at the rancho about the incident, not mentioning the fact that he knew Brick, and the gang was rather amused. None of them admired Jim Breen, but they needed his money and his protection. As Johnny Snow had told Brick, Jim Breen was a grande hombre, a big man, in Gomez Springs.

The control of Gomez Springs seemed to be vested in three men: Breen, "Lobo" Gomez, a son of his father, and Lee Duck, an unassuming yellow Chinaman, who wore yellow diamonds and a bland smile. Gomez, nicknamed the Wolf, was a big man physically, overbearing, and with a prodigious thirst for tequila. He wore a huge mustache, leather silver-trimmed shirts and the biggest sombrero in Mexico. Gomez was an ignorant bandit, but with his own following. Lee Duck was probably the smartest man in the trio, and Breen was wise enough to realize this, but to Lobo Gomez, he was just a yellow Chinaman. He knew the breed. Hadn't he smuggled dozens of them across the line?

It was the day after Brick had listened at Maxwell's window when Breen came out to the rancho. He was in bad humor, and Kelsey told Silent that a big deal had gone wrong. A little later on in the day, Lobo Gomez and two of his henchmen came along.

"Looks like a conference," grinned Kelsey. "Wonder where the Chink is?"

It was supper-time when Lee Duck came alone. He was the only one of the trio who did not affect a bodyguard.

The Breen Rancho was not a big place, and was hidden away on a little mesa-like shelf, with the only approach from the south. The builder had an eye for business and safety. It was but little over a mile from the Border, in a straight line, but impossible of approach from that direction. The buildings were of adobe, one-story, almost invisible at any distance. The ranch didn't belong to Breen. There were no boundary marks, no fences, except the corrals.

Jim Breen brought plenty of tequila along and passed it out to the boys. Silent declined. Not that he didn't drink, but he wanted to be sober enough to hear what was being said. The other boys were not particular.

It was after a venison supper, when a cold wind whirled down across the little mesa, and they gathered around the big fireplace in the low-ceiled room, sitting on crude benches or on the floor.

"You talked with Maxwell?" queried the yellow Chinaman in English.

Breen nodded sullenly, staring at the blazing mesquite roots in the fireplace.

"Talk Spanish," ordered Gomez, speaking in that tongue.

"I talked with him," replied Breen. He spoke Spanish like a Mexican.

"And he denied everything?" said Lee Duck.

"Yes."

80

"What do you believe?" asked Gomez heavily. He had eaten too much, and the heat of the fire made him drowsy.

"I don't believe Maxwell had any hand in the deal."

"If not—who did?" asked the Chinaman softly. "The hijackers did not get them. I have a way of finding out."

"Find out who they are and we will kill them," grunted Gomez.

The Chinaman smiled blandly. "My information does not cover persons—only conditions. The man who told me would be in a position to know if the hijackers got the diamonds. They did not."

Silent pricked up his ears at the word "diamonds." The Chinaman had used the English word, instead of the Spanish, and had also used "hijackers," because there is possibly no Spanish equivalent.

"What did Maxwell say?" asked Gomez.

"That the loss will ruin him."

"That is probably true," said Lee Duck.

"And that perhaps Wong Kee never sent them across," added Breen. "But Wong Kee told me he did. He gave them to Harper."

"Did he send for Harper?" queried the Chinaman.

Breen shrugged his shoulders.

"If he did," said the Chinaman, "Maxwell would possibly know why."

81

"You mean, he'd kill Harper and get the diamonds?" asked Breen.

"Harper is dead and the diamonds are gone. Wong Kee is dead, and the hijackers did not get the diamonds."

"Bring Maxwell here and we will get the truth," said Gomez. "There is a matter of many thousands to clear up."

"I can't believe that Maxwell would take them," said Breen. "He's always played square with us. His money paid for the bulk of those stones."

"Half," corrected the Chinaman.

"Breen seeks to protect Maxwell," grinned Gomez. "It is said that he is to marry Maxwell's daughter."

"You damn greaser!" snapped Breen, speaking in English, which Gomez understood but little.

The cowboys laughed, and Gomez swelled up visibly. He understood the word "greaser" very well, and any English profanity. But Breen did not fear Gomez, and sometimes he wished for a chance to kill him. The big bandit was becoming a nuisance in many ways. Breen wanted to boss Gomez Springs, without any interference.

"Nothing can be gained by quarreling," said the Chinaman softly. "This is the first reverse we have suffered."

"It was our first big chance," reminded Breen

angrily. "The rest of the deals were small compared with this. Fifty thousand dollars' worth of diamonds!"

"A hundred thousand in the States," said the Chinaman. "You say that this deal will ruin Maxwell?"

"He mortgaged his rancho to the hilt. He had no ready cash."

"Perhaps he can sell what he owns and pay up the mortgage."

"And have nothing left."

"It is of little interest to me," growled Gomez. "If Maxwell is to lose what he owns and if he has played false with us—there are many of his fat cattle in the hills and a market in Mexico."

"Damn cow-thief!" grunted Breen. "Penny-ante bandit! He ought to be picking pockets in a small town."

"Speak Spanish!" snapped Gomez.

"You spoke to me of a red-headed cowboy; the one who shot Joe Pico in Sicomoro," reminded the Chinaman.

Breen spat savagely into the fire.

"He is still there. As far as the shooting of Joe Pico was—"

"I understand that," interrupted Lee Duck. "I merely meant to say that the redhead found the body of Dell Harper. Did you ever stop to consider that *he* might have stolen the diamonds?"

"That's worth thinking about," quickly. "I

never figured him in on this. We'll have to find out what he knows about it."

"Bring him down here to me, and I'll make him tell what he knows," said Gomez. "I can make him talk. Were you not across the line the day Harper was killed?"

Breen turned his head and eyed Gomez angrily.

"You don't mean to connect me with the killing, do you?"

Gomez shrugged his shoulders.

"Some day," said Breen coldly, "there's going to be a lot of bastard Spanish spoken in hell—and you'll speak it, Gomez."

"Say that in Spanish," said Gomez.

"It's the same in any language," growled Breen.

Silent hunched against the wall, wondering what all the conversation was about. He didn't understand a word of Spanish. It was the same with Mahan, Berg, and Eddy. Kelsey understood Spanish, and after the conference broke up, and the three principals had gone back to Gomez Springs, he told them the gist of the conversation.

"This Chink named Wong Kee sent the diamonds across the line by Dell Harper, and somebody killed Harper. Wong Kee was the smart one of the gang, and never told anybody how he sent the stuff. That's how there wasn't any chance for one of the gang to double-cross the rest. Wong Kee was paid a commission on the value of the stuff; so he didn't have no interest, except to get it across safely.

"They think Maxwell got the diamonds. Anyway, Gomez and the Chink feel that way. I guess Breen is doubtful about it. Now, they've got their eye on that red-headed waddy who shot Joe Pico. He was the one who found Harper, and they think he pinched the diamonds off Harper's body. God help him if Lobo Gomez ever gets him down here. I'd hate to have that big brute lay out a torture for me."

"What was that bunch of diamonds worth?" asked Silent.

"I guess it cost them about fifty thousand, and that's only about half what the bunch would be worth across the line. Even at that, it wouldn't make a very big package."

"Fifty thousand!" exclaimed Silent. "That's money!"

"Gomez wants to raid the Maxwell rancho," laughed Kelsey. "That'll be our job, I suppose. I don't mind rustlin' cows. Anyway, yuh don't run foul of the Government, runnin' cattle. I've never hankered for a look at the inside of a Federal prison."

"Suppose they do smuggle a bunch of diamonds across the line," said Silent. "Who sells 'em?"

"Oh, they've got an agent. Didn't yuh ever

meet Sohmes? No, I guess he ain't been down here since you came. He sells 'em in Los and Frisco. Oh, there's plenty market for sparklers. I'd like to have a chance to hijack a bunch of 'em."

"You better keep that talk to yourself," advised Mahan.

"I'm not scared of Breen and Gomez. This is a game of dog eat dog down here, anyway. Some day the Mexican Government will fall in on us and line us all up against a blank wall. The newspapers in the States are all talkin' too much about this part of the country, and there'll be one grand cleanin' some day, just for the moral effect. I've been here for two years, yuh must remember."

"Have you been with Breen all that time?" asked Silent.

"Nope. I've been with Breen over a year. Some day they'll get him. He worked the smugglin' game alone for a long time, but a man double-crossed him one day, and broke Breen. The man worked the north end of the deal, and he shore cleaned Mr. Breen to the queen's taste. But Breen made another stake and joined in with Gomez and the Chink. They threw in with Maxwell and everythin' went fine until this diamond deal."

"Do you ever go across the line?" asked Silent.

"Not a chance," grinned Kelsey. "They'd grab me in a minute. Campbell knows I'm down here.

I'll bet he's got the deadwood on every one of us."

"I went across with Breen," said Silent. "We went to Sicomoro, and we saw the sheriff. In fact, Breen talked with him."

"He's got nothin' on Breen, except suspicions. Mebby he don't know who you are, Slade. Yo're lucky, if he don't."

"I'm not goin' back," seriously. "I'll take a chance down here."

"It's all right for a while," said Mahan; "but you stay down here a year or so and you'll want to go back. I've got a girl in San Berdoo."

"Daughter?" asked Silent.

"No, thank God. I never stayed still long enough to get married."

"I'd like to go back," sighed Eddy. "I've got a sister in Phoenix."

"Aw, shut up!" snapped Berg angrily. "Whinin' about home. Why didn't yuh think of it before? You've made yore own bed; so lay on it. Yo're free, at least. I don't want to spend my life down here either, but it's a damn sight better than lookin' through the bars."

"Berg's right," declared Silent. "We're danged well off, if we only know it. But I wish I could hablar Español."

"You'll get it," said Kelsey. "Get you a girl who talks it. That's how I learned."

CHAPTER V

GOMEZ SPRINGS

BRICK had been just a little worried since he had overheard the conversation between Maxwell and Breen. He did not trust Breen for a minute. Under the circumstances, the Rancho del Rosa had no protection from a raid, and Brick did not dare tell the other boys what he knew. Brick was sure that Marie did not know her father was in partnership with Jim Breen.

In fact, Brick had had little opportunity to talk with Marie since he came to work for Maxwell. He knew that Maxwell was worried. He had no way of hearing how things were going down across the line, and there was the dreadful uncertainty of what Breen, Lee Duck, and Lobo Gomez might decide to do.

Maxwell gave Slim orders to have the boys move all the cattle off the south end of the range and throw them on the north side. Brick knew he was afraid of having them stolen across the line. The boys discussed this phase of it, deciding that Maxwell had some intimation of a raid. They rather welcomed a chance for action.

Brick kept away from Sicomoro. He did not want trouble with the Pico gang. While they were moving the cattle, Brick met Berry and Mitchell, the Border Patrolmen, and Berry wanted to know if they were rounding up the cattle for shipment. Brick told him what their orders were, and Berry was interested.

"I guess I better have a talk with Maxwell," he said. "Bob is so square, he would not squeal on anybody. If he's got wind of a raid on his cattle, I want the dope on it and so does Campbell. There's men down there we'd like to catch across the Border, Davidson."

"I s'pose that's right," smiled Brick.

"There's a lot of 'wantcd' men down there," said Mitchell.

"Sort of a refuge, eh?"

"Campbell has a bunch spotted down there. Their combined rewards would make a nice stake for somebody. Campbell was tellin' me yesterday about one feller. He's dead sure it's the right man. This feller was under sentence of death away up in Montana, but he got away. Name's Slade. Campbell got the reward notice through the regular channels, I guess. There wasn't any picture, but the description sure fits the feller who was in Sicomoro a few days ago with Jim Breen. Campbell didn't think about it at the time. Mebby he's wrong, but he don't think so."

Brick's eyes hardened. It seemed as though Mitchell was telling all this for his special benefit, but before he finished Brick realized that the telling was either merely a coincidence or Berry and Mitchell were clever actors.

"I suppose they come quite a ways," said Brick.

"That's the longest trip I've heard about," laughed Mitchell. "He's worth five thousand dollars, dead or alive. Campbell is sure kickin' himself for overlookin' the chance."

Brick wondered how he could get word to Silent, warning him to keep across the line. If he and Johnny went to Gomez Springs they might see Silent, but Brick knew he would be throwing himself wide open to a lot of trouble if Breen saw him down there. Brick could see plenty trouble ahead, without hunting for it.

That afternoon Maxwell came to Brick and asked him to drive a team to Sicomoro. He told Brick that some company was coming on the stage to Sicomoro, and that he was to bring them back to the Rancho. Slim hitched the team to a two-seated buggy, and then Brick found that Marie was going with him. She climbed on the seat beside him, and they drove away from the ranch.

"I haven't had much chance to talk with you," she said, after they left the Rancho. "Dad isn't feeling well, and he seemed to want me with him most of the time. Do you like it here?"

"Yes'm, I like it fine. Yore dad is a good man to work for."

"Dad is fine. I guess everybody likes him. Do

90

you like the boys? I've noticed that you and Johnny Snow are together most of the time."

"I like Johnny fine," smiled Brick. "He's a nice, clean kid."

"He is a nice boy."

"Yeah," thoughtfully, "he's better than the average, Miss Maxwell."

"Why don't you call me Marie? Everybody else does."

"I'd like to. I'm used to callin' folks by their first name. Nobody ever calls me anything but Brick—unless they're sore at me. And that happens a lot. I reckon I'm a regular trouble hunter. That's m' red hair, I s'pose."

"Your hair *is* red," laughed Marie.

"Y'betcha. No halfway stuff with me. I started out to have red hair, and I made good. Nothin' auburn about my head, and I'll count freckles with any livin' human. They don't show so much down here, on account of this tan, but you give me a few months of winter weather, and I'll blossom out with the finest bunch of freckles yuh ever saw."

"And you have the bluest eyes I have ever seen, Brick."

"That's m' sunny disposition," laughed Brick. "I'm good-hearted, too."

"I believe you are."

"Cinch. You ain't seen our friend Breen lately, have yuh?"

Marie's eyes clouded for a moment.

"Why mention him?" she asked.

"I dunno. Every time I think of him, I think of the day he had you by the wrist. Don't never let him get yuh where yuh ain't got protection."

"Why do you say that, Brick?"

"Because he ain't to be trusted, that's why."

"He and Dad are old friends."

"That won't make no difference to Jim Breen."

"What do you know about Jim Breen?"

Brick shut his jaw tightly. He didn't want to tell her what he knew about Breen. She repeated her question.

"I can't tell yuh, Marie. You try bein' afraid of him, thasall."

Marie didn't question him further, but turned the conversation to other channels. They tied the team in front of a store, and Marie did a little shopping, while they waited for the stage. Brick didn't get far away from her. He saw the Abelardo brothers in town, and also Campbell, the sheriff. Brick would have liked to see that reward notice, offering five thousand for Silent Slade. He wondered if Harp Harris's name was on it as sheriff of Sun Dog.

Marie and Brick were standing in front of the store, when the stage came in. The tired horses came to a stop in front of the little post office, and the driver assisted the lone passenger to alight. It was a girl about the same size as Marie, and they embraced each other joyously.

Brick stayed near the buggy until after they had greeted each other, and then went over to the stage to get the baggage.

"Brick," said Marie softly, "I want you to meet Miss McKee."

Brick turned so quickly that he almost fell down. Juanita McKee was staring at him as though he was a ghost. Brick took a deep breath.

"Pleased to meetcha, Miss McKee," he said, his voice husky.

"Well," Juanita swallowed thickly, forcing a smile, "thank you."

Marie didn't notice anything wrong, but went on chattering, while Brick went to get the bags. He placed them in the buggy, and was adjusting the harness when the two girls climbed into the vehicle. Brick wondered what irony of fate ever sent Juanita McKee down in that country, until Marie explained, as they drove away.

"Juanita and I went to school together," she said. "We have always corresponded since that time, and I wanted her to come down and visit me."

"That's great," said Brick foolishly, but he didn't look around.

The two girls chattered all the way out to the Rancho. Maxwell had never met Juanita, but he gave her a friendly welcome.

"Gee, she's a good-looker!" exclaimed Johnny Snow, as he helped Brick unhitch the team. "Where's she from?"

"Marie didn't say."

"I s'pose she's engaged to some feller. That's always my luck. The next time they pull off a dance in Sicomoro, let's me and you take the two girls."

Brick smiled thinly.

"You don't exactly *hate* girls, do yuh, Brick?" asked Johnny.

"Why?"

"Don't a pretty face get yuh enthused?"

"No-o-o, I can't say it does."

"Uh-huh. Well, everybody to their tastes. What's her name?"

"McKee."

"Thasso? I wonder if she's any relation to Scotty McKee, who used to own the One Oak Cantina in Sicomoro?"

"Might be."

"Well, yo're sure interested, cowboy. When do we go down to Gomez Springs?"

"I don't know, Johnny."

"You say when."

It was later in the evening when Brick encountered Juanita on the back veranda of the ranch house.

"I've been trying to get a word alone with you," she said. "How in the world did you happen to be here?"

"It just happened," smiled Brick. "I've been here quite a little while, Juanita. It shore was a shock to see you."

"It was a shock to me," she said seriously. "Nobody in Marlin City knows where you are. Harp Harris is the sheriff now."

"And it was Harp who—you knew there was a reward for Silent?"

She nodded slowly. "They are posted up all over the country up there. The County Commissioners got them out, before they officially appointed Harp. I saw his wife before I left. She said she'd be willing for Harp to remain a deputy, if you could only come back. And Soapy Caswell came out to see me. He thinks a lot of you and Silent. When Marie wrote me to come and make her a visit, I couldn't refuse, because I wanted to get away from up there."

"I suppose they don't think much of me in Sun Dog."

"I'm afraid not, Brick. The prosecuting attorney wanted to arrest you. He didn't know you had left there. I suppose the people are about evenly divided in their feelings toward you; Mrs. Wesson says that you did just the right thing. She's a good soul."

"The best in the world, Juanita."

"Have you ever heard from Silent?"

"No," said Brick honestly, "I have never heard a word from him."

Juanita sighed deeply. "I've wondered where he is. You never thought he was guilty, did you?"

"I turned him loose, didn't I?"

"Would you have turned him loose, if he had been guilty?"

"I don't know. Yore father was dead. Nothin' could ever bring him back again; and Silent was my best friend. What is duty, anyway? Is the link of friendship so weak that a man-made duty can break it? I violated my oath of office; sacrificed my standin' with honest men. But what of it? I'm the loser—if there's any loss. The people will soon forget it; but if I had gone ahead with my duty—would I have ever forgotten it? That's my argument, Juanita."

"I know how you feel, and I've wanted to thank you. Do these people know where you are from?"

"Not exactly. I don't want them to know; because—well, I've got a chance to work out somethin' down here. I can't explain it to you."

"That's all right, Brick. I'll have to go back now, or Marie will be looking for me."

As Brick started back for the bunk-house he met a Yaqui Indian, who had slipped like a shadow into the patio, his bare feet making no sound on the old flags.

"Señor Maxwell," he said in a soft voice. "A carta."

"What kind of a cart?" asked Brick.

The Yaqui exhibited a sealed envelope.

"Oh, yeah—a carta. That must mean letter."

"Si, Señor."

Brick indicated the doorway. "You'll find him in there."

"Gracias, Señor."

Brick went on to the bunk-house, where he found Johnny Snow putting strings on an old guitar. He grinned widely.

"Goin' to serenade the girls," he said, chuckling to himself. "The rest of the bunch headed for Sicomoro."

Brick nodded and sprawled on his bunk to smoke a cigarette.

"An Injun just brought a carta to Maxwell," he said.

Johnny laughed softly, as he tested a string.

"Talkin' Español already, eh? What was he, a Yaqui?"

"I suppose so."

"Brought a letter to the old man, eh? Yuh never heard me play 'La Paloma,' didja? I can sure make yuh hear the doves. That's my only tune. Slim taught me how to play that one. He's a dinger on a guitar; plays like a Mexican."

Johnny managed to tune it, but his efforts were far from musical; so he gave up in disgust, and they played two-handed seven-up instead. Brick had been in the bunk-house about an hour when Marie came to the door, knocking timidly.

"I was afraid you might be in bed," she said when Brick opened the door, and she glanced around the room. Johnny grinned and laid down his cards.

"Where are the rest of the boys?" she asked.

"They went to town," replied Johnny. "What's the matter?"

"I don't know. Perhaps I'm foolish, but—a Yaqui brought Dad a note to-night. He put on his riding clothes and went away, without telling me where he was going, but I found the note on the floor in his room."

She handed Brick the note, which read:

Come down here at once. This is important.

BREEN.

"Gone down to Gomez Springs," said Johnny. "Why, that's all right."

"Mebby," said Brick shortly. "Mebby not, too."

"Oh, I don't know," said Marie nervously. "Something is worrying Dad all the time—and he took his gun. It always hangs in a belt near the head of his bed, but it is gone."

"Well," said Brick slowly, "me and Johnny will go down to Gomez Springs and see what we can see, Marie. I hope everythin' is all right."

"But you don't think it is, Brick."

"Well, don't you worry about him. Johnny, get yore gun."

"Is that supposed to be funny?" asked Johnny.

"I hope it will be somethin' to laugh at."

He turned to Marie. "You go to bed and don't worry. Lock every darned door tight, and don't come outside until we tell yuh it's us."

"What's the idea?" queried Johnny quickly.

"Just my idea of humor. C'mon, Sancho Panza."

"That sounds like a Spanish cuss word," said Johnny, as they trotted back to the stable.

"It ain't," laughed Brick. "Sancho Panza was the silent partner of a feller named Don Kiote, who went out to spear a windmill."

"Is that what you're goin' to do?"

"Somethin' like that, I reckon. Better pick a fast bronc, 'cause we might want to come north pretty danged fast."

"Don't tell me about that. Didn't me and Slim rescue a Dutchman?"

They saddled swiftly and rode away from the rancho. The road from Sicomoro to Gomez Springs ran past the Rancho del Rosa; so they headed due south at a swift gallop. Only a couple of monuments, invisible at night, marked the boundary line, but Johnny told Brick when they were out of the States.

They slowed down a little, but there was little conversation. They did not meet any one in that three-mile ride from the Border. Johnny knew the town very well, and Brick explained that they had better leave their horses in a secluded spot, but where they could get at them fairly quick, in case of emergency.

Johnny led the way and they tied their horses away from the main street, but not over a long block from the big cantina and gambling house. They sauntered easily around to the main street, which was not over two blocks long. No one paid any attention to them.

They crossed the street and approached the big cantina. There were no curtains on the dirty windows. Men were going in and out of the place, and other men lounged around the entrance, all conversing in Spanish. Brick and Johnny, their sombreros drawn low over their faces, loitered at a window long enough to see Bob Maxwell and Jim Breen at the bar.

But while the two cowboys were watching, the two men left the bar and crossed the room to a stairway at the left.

"Gone up to a room," grunted Brick. "I wish I had a chance to hear what was said."

"Let me get some of this straight," whispered Johnny. "What's all the fuss about the old man comin' down here? What's the danger?"

Brick motioned for him to follow, and they circled the rear of the building. It was dark around there, but Brick found that there was an outside stairway, which led to a rear door on the second story. It was a temptation for Brick to sneak up that stairway, but he decided to stay where he was and play safe for a while.

"Here's the old man's horse," whispered

Johnny. It was tied to an old fence near the rear door.

They moved ahead to where they could look down an alley to the main street, but came back to the rear of the cantina again, where they sat down against the corner of the adjoining building, and Brick told Johnny what he knew about Bob Maxwell, and about the missing diamonds.

"Well, didja ever see such hair on a dog!" snorted Johnny. "How much of that didja hear from the ladder the other night?"

"Enough to make me afraid of what might happen to Maxwell."

"I'll be a liar!" breathed Johnny. "The old man a smuggler!"

"Sh-h-h-h!" whispered Brick.

Some one had opened the upper doorway, and the hinges creaked. Some one was whispering. Came the soft shuffle of feet on the stairway, the grunt of some one carrying a heavy burden, the creak of the stairs.

"That last drink shore got him," said a voice softly.

"Shut up!" hissed a voice. "Are you sure there's a rope on his saddle?"

"Hold up his feet. Where's that damn horse?"

A man laughed breathlessly. Brick and Johnny froze against the side of the building. They were not over thirty feet from the horse.

"Whoa!" grunted a voice. "Somebody hold that horse, will you?"

Came the hiss of a rope, subdued conversation for several moments.

"That's good; he won't come off. You stay here, Berg, while we get the rest of the horses."

"He's too drunk," said another. "Oh, well, you're the boss."

Three men passed within six feet of Brick and Johnny, and they could see their dark bulk against the light from the street as they went down the alley.

Brick squeezed Johnny's arm, as a signal to stay where he was, and got cautiously to his feet. As noiselessly as possible he stepped across the alley, where he bumped into the wall, swore huskily, and came stumbling around the corner. There was no attempt to go silently now. Brick was playing drunk in the dark.

"Que es?" asked Berg, as Brick came stumbling toward him.

"Buenas noches," said Brick thickly. It was the one greeting he remembered just then.

"Go on back, you drunken bum," growled Berg. "Vamos!"

Came the sound of a dull blow, a grunt of surprise, then Brick's voice, speaking softly:

"Johnny! All set, Kid."

CHAPTER VI

THE ABELARDOS CALL UPON BRICK

IT was possibly ten minutes later when the three men came back. One was Jim Breen, another was Lobo Gomez, and the third was Silent Slade. Berg did not answer their hail. Everything was all right, except that Berg was not there.

"He got thirsty," said Silent. Breen swore, but said nothing more. He took the lead rope, and they headed for the Breen Ranch, two miles away.

"It was a clever scheme," said Gomez, riding beside Breen. "We'll make him talk, eh? Oh, he will talk very much. Leave it to Gomez."

"No wonder they call you Lobo; always looking for blood. And I wonder how much you could spill of your own before you turned yellow."

"No man could make a Gomez cry for mercy," boastingly.

"I suppose not. I've seen men go so yellow that they couldn't speak. But I don't think you would be that way, Lobo; you are never without words."

"I am a Gomez."

Silent was getting a smattering of Spanish, but was unable to follow the conversation. He knew that the gang suspected Maxwell of playing

103

crooked with them, and that they were going to force him to tell the truth. Breen had cleverly given Maxwell enough knockout drops to keep him asleep for an hour. It was the safest way to take Maxwell out to the ranch. Silent didn't mind playing the game with Breen. Maxwell meant nothing to Silent, but he had understood enough to know that they were going to torture Maxwell, in case he refused to talk. Silent wondered if he could stand there and watch such a thing.

But what else could he do, he wondered? He was outlawed from the United States. Where could he go, in case he started trouble with Breen and his gang? His best policy was to play the game with them until something better presented itself.

They traveled rather swiftly, because Breen was anxious to hear what Maxwell would have to say, and the two miles were covered in a short time. Eddy, Kelsey, and Mahan were at the ranch when they came in, and crowded outside when Breen called to them.

Gomez and Silent took the ropes off their victim, and between them they carried him into the living-room, placing him on the floor.

"Madre de Dios!" roared Gomez. "Mira!"

It was Berg, the outlaw, not Bob Maxwell.

Breen starcd down at poor Berg, who was just recovering. His head was bleeding from a scalp wound, which had swollen badly.

"What in hell?" roared Breen, looking vacantly around. He grasped Silent by the arm, bracing himself. Lobo Gomez laughed foolishly and crossed himself.

"What's the idea?" queried Mahan coldly. "Who hit Berg?"

"I wish I—I—" Breen shook his head. "Oh, I don't know. What kind of a hocus-pocus is this? What do you say?" he asked Silent.

"Somethin'," said Silent slowly, "must have happened."

"What's the matter?" asked Berg painfully, feeling of his head.

"What happened to you?" demanded Breen. "Don'tcha remember, Berg? We left you behind the cantina. Remember that?"

Berg squinted painfully. He didn't remember anything, because his head was aching, and he wanted a drink. Mahan handed him a bottle of tequila and he lowered it two inches at one swallow. It braced him up a little, and they helped him on an old cot.

"Remember what happened?" asked Breen.

"I'm kinda hazy about it," said Berg. "There was a drunken man. He came through the alley in the dark. I didn't see him. I—I asked him who it was and he said good-night. Then somethin' hit me."

"You show that," grunted Breen. He sank down in a chair near the fire, holding his head in his hands, trying to puzzle out who had made the substitution. Lobo Gomez paced up and down the room, his big spurs raking loudly across the rough floor. Mahan gave Breen the tequila bottle, and Berg proceeded to forget his part of the affair.

"Who was it?" asked Gomez. "Who took Maxwell off that horse? With my own hands I tied those ropes. Who knew Maxwell came to the cantina?"

"Ask yourself a few questions," snarled Breen. "How do I know?"

"What did the Yaqui tell you?"

"He said he gave Maxwell the letter, and that no one saw them leave."

"Who in Gomez Springs is Maxwell's friend?"

"Stop asking questions! We've lost our chance to get Maxwell. He'll never come down here again—unless we bring him."

"Then we will bring him."

"Fool!"

"Why am I a fool? One man is easily handled."

"Go up there and try it. Maxwell will be on his guard now. His own men would—" Breen paused thoughtfully. "I wonder if any of Maxwell's men were in Gomez Springs to-night? I must find out. I'll question that Yaqui again. Let's go back to town; we can do nothing here."

Albert and William Abelardo, half-breed Spanish and negro, were a hard pair. They owned a small herd of cattle and a tumble-down ranch-house a couple of miles north of Sicomoro. Albert was thin, scrawny, with a loose-lipped mouth, crooked nose and shifty eyes. When loaded down with his Sunday clothes, he would weigh about a hundred and twenty.

William was short and squat, with a flat nose, thin lips, and a mustache, which grew thin on one side, possibly due to a deep scar on his upper lip, giving his face a lop-sided appearance. He would weigh about a hundred and sixty. They were not only mean, but they were ignorantly mean.

Their paternal ancestor had been a brother to Mrs. Pico, which made them cousins of the Pico tribe. They rather adored Edward Pico, because he controlled the liquor trade of Sicomoro, and they were willing to follow out his orders and advice.

They knew all about Brick Davidson shooting Joe Pico. It had been like a slap in the face to them. Were they not cousins of Joe? A blow at any of the Pico family was a blow to them. It was all settled between them that they were going to kill Brick. Remained only the opportunity.

This night they got drunk. It was not an unusual occurrence. Then they went down to visit Joe, who was convalescent. The sight of poor Joe, lying there, his face very white—that is, white for one of his color—whetted their imagination.

"Sure, I keel theese radhad," said Al. He loved to talk English.

"I'm keel some herself," declared Bill, whose English was not of the best. "I keel heem firs' chance you get."

"Damn fool!" spat Al. "You spik English like Swid."

Al had known one Swede in his life—a sheep-herder.

"I'm keel pretty dead," insisted Bill.

"One dead is jus' like two," declared Al intelligently. "You fill all right, Joe?"

Joe coughed dismally. He had no sense of humor, and these two well-meaning cousins always made his head ache.

"You see?" said Bill. "Theese Joe Pico dam seek. Make bad noise in hees neck. Good-bye, Joe."

"Go to hell!" grunted Joe, as they stumbled out of the room.

"W'ere we go now?" asked Al.

"Go get more drink. I'm sad for Joe."

"You theenk he's go to die?"

"Sure t'ing. Hell! W'y ask me that? Can't you see from your eye?"

"Um-m-m-m. He's die pretty good all right. Poor Joe! Let's drink."

They drank tequila at the One Oak Cantina, procured a bottle to take along, and mounted their horses.

"We get even on theese radhad for shoot Joe," declared Al. "These Maxwell puncher all to town theese night."

"Buena!" exclaimed Bill, exhilarated by a big drink of the potent juice of the maguey plant. "I'm feel from yall—me."

"You yall and I'm knock hell from you. Theese ees quiet job."

"Sure! We call heem out—bam! Radhad ees mucho muerto. Ver' good."

"Um-m-m-m," agreed Al. It had suddenly dawned upon him that it might be dangerous to murder Brick. He remembered that they hanged murderers. Hanging was an unpleasant way to pass out; so he patiently explained the idea to Bill, who was getting quite drunk.

"He shoot Joe," declared Bill. "Nobody hang from theese."

"Joe re'ch for hees gon, Beel. There ees difference."

"Buena! We mak' radhad re'ch for hees gon."

"Huh!" disgustedly. "You want die? Let's have dreenk."

They had the drink.

"Theese radhad mus' be on rancho," said Al huskily.

"Mus' be," agreed Bill. He didn't know why the redhead must be on the ranch, except that Al had so declared. They went on.

· · ·

Marie and Juanita did not go to bed. They locked all the doors and waited for the return of Brick and Johnny. Juanita couldn't understand what it was all about, because Marie didn't know. She explained about the murder of Dell Harper, and told her of Brick's fight with Joe Pico in Sicomoro. Juanita thrilled at Marie's description of what had happened in the patio, when Jim Breen had grasped her by the wrist.

"I really believe Brick would have shot him, Juanita," she said.

"He certainly would. I mean, he looks like a person who would shoot."

"He proved it in Sicomoro. Joe Pico is a dangerous man. They say he is very fast with a gun. I'm sorry for Brick's sake that it happened."

"Perhaps he can take care of himself."

"I'm sure he can, but it isn't a case of watching one man. The Pico gang have always been trouble-makers. Edward Pico owns all the cantinas in Sicomoro, and he rules a certain element. Dad says they are hijackers. The worst of the gang are the Abelardo brothers. If the truth were known they'd probably both be hung in short order."

"But I don't understand why your father should be in any danger. You say that he and Breen are old, old friends."

Marie shook her head thoughtfully. "I don't

know. Ever since the murder of Dell Harper, Dad has been worried about something. He's aged years in a few days. I've never known Dad to carry a gun until now. He tries to appear cheerful, but I know he is afraid of something. It is true that Dad and Jim Breen have been friends for a long time.

"Dad wanted me to marry Jim Breen. I used to like Jim, but I never cared to have him for a husband. I heard Slim say one day that Breen smokes marahuana. I didn't believe that until the day Brick came, and Jim Breen almost twisted my wrist off. If he wasn't drunk on marahuana, he was crazy, because he was far from being normal."

Juanita was staring at the wall, her hands on the arm of her chair. Jim Breen of Gomez Springs! Marahuana weed! It came back to her now. She remembered that Brick had talked with her about the envelope he had found in their ranch house near the body of her father. And the little tobacco sack, containing a few crumbs of marahuana weed.

"What in the world is the matter?" asked Marie anxiously.

Juanita blinked at her. It was very quiet around the rancho, when suddenly came the clicking of hoofs on the flags of the patio. Marie sprang to her feet and ran to the door, unlocking it quickly.

"They've come back!" she exclaimed, as she

111

tugged at the big key. "Oh, I hope they've brought good news."

Flinging the door open, she ran out on the back porch. There was no moon, and everything was very dark in the patio.

"Brick!" she called softly. Juanita came to the doorway, peering out in the darkness.

"I'm sure I heard horses," said Juanita, coming out beside Marie.

"It's so dark out here." Came a soft rustling in the bushes beside the porch, and they turned to look into the evil face of Albert Abelardo. He had a gun in his right hand, pointing straight at them, a grin on his loose lips. He stepped between them and the doorway.

"What do you want?" asked Marie.

Al blinked owlishly.

"W'ere's radhad?"

"Who?"

"Radhad. Madre de Dios, can' you onnerstan from English?"

"Redhead," whispered Juanita.

"He isn't here," said Marie. Bill Abelardo stumbled against the steps, as he came up to them, and swore roundly in Spanish.

"Not 'ere, eh?" growled Al. Even filled with tequila, he was no fool.

"I'm wan' talk to man," he said. "Damn women!"

"There's no men—" Marie stopped. "You better go back home."

Al laughed drunkenly.

"Beel," he said laughing huskily, "she's say no man 'ere. Theese ees luck, eh? Let's all have dreenk."

"Bonito muchacha, mucho tequila," laughed Bill joyfully. "Pretty girls and much tequila."

"Don't you dare go in that house," warned Marie. "Go back home, you drunken idiots! If my father ever catches you here—"

"Who you geeve theese order to, huh?" demanded Al. "You know from who you talk?"

The gun in Al's hand waved drunkenly, the hammer at full cock. Marie and Juanita backed through the doorway, and Marie tried to slam the door in their faces, but Al blocked it, and they followed the girls in. Bill kicked the door shut, and drew the bottle from inside his shirt.

"No dreenk jus' now," ordered Al. He turned to Marie. "I'm wan' see radhad," thickly. "He shoot Joe."

"Yes, and he'll shoot you, if he catches you here," said Juanita.

"Quien sabe?" shrugging his shoulders drunkenly. Then—"Who de hell are you? I'm not see you biffore? Pretty girl, eh? Theese one," he pointed at Marie, who was edging toward the stairway, "belong to Breen. Ha, ha, ha, ha! Damn Breen! Some day I cut out hees leever. I am Abelardo."

"Si—Abelardo!" grunted Bill. "Ver' mucho

damn fool! You put theese cork so deep in theese bottle—"

"Idiota!" snapped Al. "Leave cork alone."

"Sure. So damn deep—"

"Diablo!" yelled Al, and Bill dropped the bottle on his toes.

Marie had skipped up the stairs, and Al, interested in Juanita, had barely seen the sudden exit. He started on a run for the stairs, tripped over a rumpled rug, and went sprawling, his revolver exploding with a jarring thud, the bullet smashing through the lift of the lower step.

Al got slowly to his feet, dazed, while Bill exploded with mirth. Juanita was frightened, and backed against the wall, but she didn't lose her presence of mind.

"You better go quickly," she said in Spanish. "Marie has gone to get a shotgun."

Bill rubbed the back of a dirty hand across his mouth. He was still sober enough to realize that there might be truth in this. And Bill did not relish shotguns. Al swore savagely, and they both started for the door at the same time.

Juanita, hardly knowing what she was doing, picked up the bottle of tequila and flung it as hard as she could toward the doorway, where Al and Bill were going out, side by side, and the heavy bottle landed with a dull *cluck!* on the back of Bill's head, and Bill went sprawling.

• • •

Brick and Johnny had little trouble in getting Maxwell away from Gomez Springs. They carried him around to their horses, swung him up on Brick's saddle, while Brick rode behind, and they went swiftly back along the road. Johnny was breathless until they reached the Border.

Bob Maxwell was unconscious, and Brick had difficulty in keeping him in the saddle.

"Oh, but there'll be plenty cussin' in Mexico," laughed Johnny. "Wish I could see that gang when they find one of their own men on that horse. Who was he, do yuh suppose?"

"He didn't introduce himself," laughed Brick.

"Do yuh think yuh killed him?"

"Well, I hit him hard enough, if that's what yuh mean. Any time yuh have to strike in the dark— make it a good one, Johnny."

"Well, it almost ruined my nerves. I shore was scared."

They didn't meet anybody on the way back to the rancho, for which Brick was thankful. He knew that the Border officers watched that road pretty closely, and he didn't want to explain anything to them.

They rode into the patio and Brick saw the bulky outlines of two horses. None of their gang would leave horses in the patio.

"Look out, Johnny!" he called sharply. "Some-body here."

Brick slid off quickly, eased Maxwell to the

ground, and stepped around the horse. Johnny's horse swung around as he started to dismount. Came the smashing report of a shotgun from an upper window, the horse whirled quickly, and Johnny went sprawling.

Brick was running toward the doorway, which had just opened, letting a beam of light across the porch, and he crashed into Al Abelardo, who went staggering back into the light. Brick recognized him in a flash, and without any preliminary motions, he sprang ahead, lashed out with a fist, which caught Al on that angle of his chin known in ring parlance as the "button," and Al went down in a heap. Brick jumped back toward the doorway, almost falling over Bill.

"Marie!" he called. "Marie, where are you?"

"She's upstairs, Brick," answered Juanita in a weak voice.

Johnny came up on the porch, panting heavily, and they went into the house. Juanita was leaning against a table, her face white in the light from the big oil lamp.

Marie was coming down the stairs, leaning forward to get a clear view of the room. She came on down, staring at Brick and Johnny.

"We've had company," said Juanita blankly.

"I see yuh did," replied Brick. "I met one of 'em as I came in."

"I—I hit the other with a bottle," said Juanita weakly.

"Them damn Abelardo brothers!" snorted Johnny indignantly. "Wait'll I get a rope."

He ran back, untied his lariat from the saddle, and came back to the doorway. Al was trying to sit up, mumbling foolishly, but Johnny shoved him down again, as he roped them together.

Brick went over to Marie. She was trembling a little.

"What did you—did you find out anything, Brick?"

"I've got yore dad out in the patio, Marie. No, he's all right. They gave him knockout drops, I reckon, but he'll soon sleep them off. You girls fix a bed for him, will yuh?"

Brick and Johnny brought him in and placed him on the bed. He was snoring lustily, which reassured the girls to some extent. They left him and went back to the main room, where Marie and Juanita told of their experiences with the Abelardo brothers.

Johnny seemed nervous. He walked aimlessly about the room, while Brick told them what had happened at Gomez Springs.

"But what is it all about?" wondered Marie. "Why would they do this to my dad? What was their idea in putting him to sleep and trying to take him away? I don't understand. Did Jim Breen do it, Brick?"

"I reckon he did. Mebby yore dad will explain things, when he wakes up. I reckon the danger is all over for to-night. The boys ought to be back pretty soon, but don't tell them anythin' about it."

"Why? Do you think Dad has done anything wrong?"

"That would depend entirely on who answered the question. You girls go to bed and get some sleep. Nothin' to worry about now."

"What are you going to do with those two men?" asked Juanita.

"What'll we do with 'em, Jumpin' Jack?" asked Brick. Johnny stopped pacing the room.

"Oh, I'm glad I didn't hit any one with that shotgun," said Marie. "I heard the door open and I realized that they had gone out, but I just poked the gun out of the window and fired one shot at random."

Johnny flinched noticeably and walked over to the door.

"I reckon we better talk things over with these fellers," he said.

Brick grinned, told the girls good-night, and closed the door behind them. Both Al and Bill were conscious, partly sober and very contrite.

"We go home now," said Bill. "We hurt nobody."

"That's fine," said Brick. "But you tough eggs better get yore lesson, 'cause the teacher is goin' to be severe. What'll we do with 'em?"

"Hang the pair of 'em," said Johnny savagely. "Go find a tall limb and give the buzzards a feed."

118

"That's an idea," laughed Brick. "A little hangin' will do 'em good."

And in spite of their protests, they were roped to their horses, and the cavalcade started toward Sicomoro. Al Abelardo showed a disposition to call upon all the saints to witness a great wrong to his family, but Bill retained a dogged silence. That tequila bottle was rather hard.

About a mile from the rancho, a huge oak flung its gnarled limbs across the dusty road, and here they stopped. The ceremony was brief. A rope was knotted beneath the arms of each man, the loose end thrown over a big limb, and tied off to a lower one. Al prayed fervently. He didn't realize that the rope was not around his neck until the horse went from under him. Bill screamed once, and then began to swear, when he found himself dangling six feet above the road.

"I reckon that'll remind 'em of their many sins," laughed Brick, as they mounted and turned their horses back toward the rancho. "How do yuh feel, Johnny?"

"My name is Random," seriously.

"What?"

"Random."

"Yea-a-ah? What's the idea?"

"Marie said she shot at random, didn't she? That's me."

"Yuh mean—she hit yuh?"

"I didn't set down in the house, did I? I've stood up in my stirrups ever since we left the ranch, ain't I? Holee-e-e cats! I feel like I been settin' in a cactus. You borry a pair of tweezers from Marie, will yuh. Tell her yuh got a sliver."

"I'll do it, Mr. Random."

"That may be funny to you, but it ain't to me. I'm so full of them little ball-bearings that I'd roll right off a chair. This has been a full night for old man Snow's little gift to humanity."

It was well past midnight when Slim Neeley, Buck Eads, and Leo Herrera came back from Sicomoro. Brick and Johnny were in their bunks, when Buck lighted the lamp, and they heard him choking with laughter.

"Laugh, yuh danged fool!" exploded Slim. "Funny, ain't it?"

Brick and Johnny sat up in their blankets.

"What's the idea of all the noise?" queried Johnny.

"Look at Slim, will yuh?"

Slim had blood on his nose, and one eye was swelled shut. He had put on his Sunday suit, a light blue creation—and it was a mess.

"Fightin' again, eh?" queried Johnny.

Buck doubled up with mirth and Slim kicked at him.

"Who did yuh kill, Slim?" asked Brick.

"This is Sandy Claws," choked Buck. "He took a present off the tree."

120

"Danged laughin' hyena! Look at my new suit!"

Buck sat down on the edge of a bunk and tried to control his mirth long enough to tell Brick and Johnny what happened.

"We was comin' home," explained Buck. "It's darker than hell along the road. We're out here about a mile, jist goin' along kinda poco-poco, when all to once Slim lets out a grunt, and I hear an awful noise, jist as though he was in mortal combat.

"His horse jumps sideways and almost knocks my horse down, and then I hear a whopper of a thump on the ground. *Wham!* Somethin' hit me, but I ducked quick and fell off in the road. There's Leo, squallin': 'Que es? Que es?' and a horse almost stepped on me. I says: 'What the hell was it, Slim?' and Slim says: 'Gloffwupp sloggeruff.'"

"My mouth was full of dust," said Slim painfully.

"Well," chuckled Buck, "as soon as Slim told me what it was, I knowed what we was up against. I thought the Russian army had attacked us. I hate to shoot in the dark; so I lit a match. There's Slim, flat in the dust, with his arms around Al Abelardo, and jist above my head hangs Bill Abelardo, staring down at the light. There's a hunk of busted maguey hangin' over the limb and—"

"The dirty bum kicked me in the face," complained Slim, "and then I grabbed him around the legs and the rope busted."

"What was they doin' up there in the tree?" asked Johnny.

"Hangin'," grinned Buck. "It's a fact. I dunno whether somebody tied 'em up there, or whether that's their natcheral way to go to sleep. They didn't know. I told 'em to do their hangin' away from the main road next time. We cut Bill down, took off their ropes, and gave 'em both a good swift kick in the pants."

"That's a funny way to sleep," said Brick.

"Ain't it? If somebody hung them up there, they made an awful mistake; they should have put the ropes around their dirty necks."

"I'm goin' to bust into the kitchen and find me a hunk of raw meat for my eye," said Slim.

"Is yore name Random?" asked Johnny.

"Random? What's wrong with you? You know damn well it ain't."

"Go ahead—yo're safe."

"What's achin' that pop-eyed waddy?" wondered Slim.

"You'd be terribly surprised to know."

"Yo're all elbows to-night," complained Brick.

"Gotta do somethin' with 'em, Brick. When yo're sleepin' on yore face, yuh can't let yore arms trail out behind yuh."

CHAPTER VII

MAXWELL TALKS

IT was the following morning just after breakfast, and the boys were leaving the table, when Marie, standing in the doorway, signaled to Brick. He left the boys and came back to her.

"Dad wants to see you," she said.

"Oh, all right. How is he this mornin'?"

"I don't think he feels very well."

Brick followed her up to Maxwell's room, where they found him in bed. He looked old and tired, with bloodshot eyes and dry lips. The big dose of knockout drops had nearly finished him. He smiled weakly and motioned for Brick to sit down.

"I have talked things over with Marie," he told Brick. "She has told me what occurred here last night, and I want to thank you for everything. It is a small thing to do—to merely thank you, Davidson. I feel that perhaps you saved my life, and who knows what might have happened if you hadn't come back here at the opportune time?"

He stared at the ceiling for several moments, his eyes half-closed.

"Davidson, you are a stranger here. You don't understand conditions, and perhaps you don't understand the people along this Border. All of my life I have lived here. My father and his father owned the Rancho del Rosa. My grandfather was a Don."

He said it proudly, but there was a catch in his voice.

"Dishonor was unknown in those days. A man's honor was above everything else. It was twenty miles across the Rancho del Rosa, granted by the King of Spain to the first Maxwell here. I am not boasting. Twenty years ago I inherited this place, and I have wasted my heritage; thrown it away over the green cloth and the race tracks.

"There were times when I was unable to pay my taxes, and the State took land in lieu of gold, until the Rancho has dwindled to a mere handful of acres, instead of thousands. I could see it going. I am not a fool, even though I may be a knave. You wonder why I am telling you this? It is because you brought me home last night; because I think you are entitled to know why certain things were done.

"I wanted money, Davidson; more money than this place could pay me. I had lived here a long time, and I have seen big money made. Men have become rich in a short while; dishonest riches, it is true, but riches. I am not boasting when I say that no man on this Border would ever suspect me. I have the confidence of the Border officers.

"Certain men knew this, and they came to me.

No matter who they are. I am not incriminating anybody. It was a fascinating game. Even the hijackers would never suspect me. My foreman was let into the game, and before that he was as square as a dollar. Then came a chance to pick up a wonderful lot of unset diamonds.

"A diamond expert was sent into Mexico to appraise them. The price was but a small part of their value, once we had them across the line, but it was more than we could afford. I could see a chance to retrieve a fortune at one throw; so I mortgaged the Rancho del Rosa for every cent I could get, and we bought the diamonds."

Maxwell paused for several moments, his hands clutching the blanket.

"Wong Kee sent them across the line by Dell Harper, and somebody killed Harper," said Brick thoughtfully. "And then Wong Kee got killed in a fan-tan game. That's a queer twist of fate, ain't it?"

Maxwell stared at Brick wonderingly. His eyes shifted to Marie, but came quickly back to Brick's freckled face and serious blue eyes.

"You knew this?" he asked hoarsely. "Who are you, Davidson? Are you a Government spy?"

"I'm jist a cow-puncher," smiled Brick. "Mebby I've got an axe to grind, but it ain't got anythin' to do with you, Mr. Maxwell. I knew that Jim Breen and his gang think that you got away with those diamonds, and I figured they was takin' you somewhere to make yuh tell. Me and Johnny Snow found yore horse behind the cantina; so we waited, and heard them tie yuh on yore horse. They left one man in charge, while they got their horses; so I popped him over the head and put him in yore place. Now, how much did they tell yuh before yuh got the doped drink?"

"Not a thing. We were to go up to Breen's private room to talk over things, and he served a drink. It tasted all right, but I had no more than swallowed it when everything went spinning around. And then I don't remember a thing until I woke up here with a splitting headache, and found Marie putting cold compresses on my head."

"They shore handed you a good one. I'll bet they're worried now."

"Worried!" Maxwell shut his eyes. "The fools think I killed Dell Harper, when I loved him like a son. I got him into this. He would have been honest, but I needed him to help me be a crook. I've told you my story—but you seem to have known it."

"Well," smiled Brick, "you ain't the first good man to go wrong. Yo're payin' the price, Mr. Maxwell; and it ain't what you'd call a sale. Do you think Wong Kee played square?"

"I do."

"How about Jim Breen? Suppose Jim Breen

knowed that Harper was to bring the diamonds across? You remember, Breen was here that day."

"You mean that Breen might have killed Harper and taken the diamonds? Oh, I can't believe that. I've known Jim Breen for—"

"You turned smuggler because you was above reproach, remember."

"That is true. But I can't believe that Breen would do a thing like that. I don't believe *anybody* knew when and how those diamonds were to come across, except Wong Kee. He was a wizard in scheming out new ways. Harper never went over there on purpose to smuggle anything."

"Breen hates you, Davidson. Look out for him. Keep out of Mexico and keep your eyes open here, because you wounded Joe Pico. I think the Pico gang are hijackers, and I think they got the diamonds. The Abelardo brothers are two of the gang."

"What did you do with them last night?" asked Marie.

"Hung 'em up on a tree," chuckled Brick. "Tied a rope under their arms, ran the rope over a limb, and left 'em danglin' over the road. Didn't yuh notice Slim's black eye this mornin'? We hung 'em over the road, and the boys ran into 'em in the dark. I think Al Abelardo kicked Slim in the eye. The boys cut 'em down and booted 'em toward town. It was sort of a weak finish for a couple of bad men, don'tcha think?"

Maxwell tried to smile.

"Marie told me about firing the shotgun, and it was fortunate that no one got hit."

Brick looked at Marie and chuckled.

"I plumb forgot to bring back yore tweezers," he told her. "I took fifteen shot out of Johnny, before we went to bed last night."

Marie sprang to her feet.

"My God!" she exclaimed. "I didn't hit Johnny, did I?"

"Yes'm, I reckon he got into the outside edge of that pattern."

Marie was running down the stairs, before Brick finished. She went out across the back veranda and into the patio. Johnny Snow was watering his horse at the old well, and he looked at her in amazement, as she stopped a few feet away, looking at him.

"Johnny!" she panted, "Brick just told me. Where did I shoot you?"

Johnny's ears grew red and he shifted his feet nervously. Then—

"Well!" slowly, "I took my stirrups up three notches this mornin'."

Then he picked up his rope and led the horse back toward the stables, while Marie stared after him. She walked back to the veranda, a puzzled frown between her eyes. Brick came out through the doorway, and she looked up.

"Did I really hit him?" she asked anxiously.

"Didn't he admit it?"

"No, he merely said that he took up his stirrups three—o-o-o-oh!"

Marie understood. She flushed quickly, turned, and ran toward the door, while Brick grinned widely and went on out to the stable, where he found Johnny waiting for him.

"You told her," accused Johnny. "You told her she shot me."

"But I didn't tell her where. Anyway, I think she ought to know she hit somethin'. It shore is discouragin' to think that yuh can't hit anythin', even with a shotgun. Now she'll have more confidence in herself."

"Brick," solemnly, "do yuh really think she's sorry?"

"I really think she is. I had a long talk with Maxwell, and he spilled the whole works. He's busted—or danged near it. Every cent he owned was in that diamond deal. Personally, I think Jim Breen killed Harper and stole the diamonds for himself—but Maxwell don't believe it."

"By golly, I do! I'll betcha Breen is pullin' all this makin'-Maxwell-talk stuff to square himself with the rest of the gang. Dang him, he knows where the diamonds are. I'd like to find him with his head caught, and me with a baseball bat—I'll bet he'd admit somethin'.

"And another thing—me and you better look out for the Pico and Abelardo factions. They was

129

just a couple of drunken bums last night, and they squalled like rabbits, but they're side-winders, jist the same. Marie said they was lookin' for you. If things hadn't broke the way they did, you might have had to kill 'em both."

"That," said Brick seriously, "would have shore caused me a lot of sleepless nights. Dad always told me to never sass a fool or fight a cripple."

"They may be fools, but they ain't cripples."

"I'll betcha the one Slim picked off the tree is this mornin'," laughed Brick. "Gosh, that shore was funny. The boys are still wonderin' who hung 'em up, I suppose."

"Do you mean the Abelardo boys?"

"No—our boys. Oh, I reckon the Abelardo boys knew who we were."

"Yo're danged right they did, and they're notchin' bullets right now. If Breen and his gang knew who switched loads on him last night, me and you are in for a sweet time."

"Well, he'd have a hunch that it wasn't any enemy of Maxwell's. And he'd realize that Maxwell will fight shy of him from now on. This old friendship stuff is all off, and the next time Breen comes across the Border, he'll come with blood in his eye. What's Slim's orders this mornin'?"

"We're brandin' calves down on Old Adobe Creek. Maxwell wants all them cows thrown on the north side, and Slim thought we'd better do our calf-brandin' down at the old corral this mornin', rather than to bring the bunch up here and hold 'em."

Brick nodded and turned toward the stable door.

"I was just wonderin' if we ought to all go away from here, under the circumstances."

"Oh, it's all right in the daytime," replied Johnny. "And we don't want to have to explain to Slim and the rest. He asked me this mornin' why I was makin' my stirrups so short."

"What did you tell him?"

"Oh, I jist told him that if a feller ever wanted to be anythin' in the world he'd have to be different than the rest. He wanted to know if that's why I had quit workin' for a livin'. Go git yore horse, and I'll show yuh how to stand up and save saddle-leather."

CHAPTER VIII

BREEN MAKES ANOTHER PLAY

HUBERT SOHMES was ostensibly a diamond merchant of San Francisco. He dealt in large quantities of unset diamonds which had never paid any duty, and waxed wealthy thereby. He was of medium height, rather inclined to fleshiness, baldness, and horn-rimmed glasses. He was quite a traveler. In fact, he came to Mexico rather often, although this was the first time he had ever been to the Rancho del Rosa.

It was Sohmes who had appraised the diamonds which were missing, and as he had invested ten thousand in their purchase, he was naturally concerned over the reasons why they had never been delivered to him. And it was Sohmes who had placed the mortgage for Maxwell, paying for it himself on Breen's recommendation.

Breen had an eye on the Rancho del Rosa, feeling that in case Maxwell did lose it he might make an easy deal with Sohmes. Breen knew that Maxwell would never part with the Rancho, except to lose it outright on a gamble.

Sohmes wanted those diamonds. He had a buyer for the lot, and he came down to see just why they had never been placed in his hands. Neither Breen nor Maxwell had notified him of the loss, because neither of them felt that they could trust such a message on paper, and they had never made up any code words.

Bob Maxwell didn't know Sohmes, except by name. It was the third day after Maxwell's experience in Gomez Springs that Sohmes drove out from Sicomoro, hiring a Mexican from the livery-stable to drive the rig. After Sohmes had introduced himself to Maxwell, he said he came out there to get his information, rather than to cross the line to Gomez Springs.

"The Border Patrol might wonder why I went there," he told Maxwell, as they sat down in Maxwell's room. "Breen assured me that I would have the stones long before this, and I wanted him to know that a certain buyer is anxious to get them, and at a good price. It will be a quick deal, and with a good profit to all of us."

"How much did you have invested in those diamonds, Sohmes?" asked Maxwell.

"Ten thousand dollars. Why do you say 'did have'?" quickly.

"Because they're gone—vanished."

"Ridiculous!" Sohmes jerked to his feet. "You don't mean to sit there and tell me—"

"Sit down."

Sohmes slowly sat down, staring at Maxwell, blinking his eyes behind the glasses, licking his rather thick lips, while Maxwell told him the story.

"But—but—" spluttered Sohmes. "I lose ten thousand dollars!"

"And I lose the Rancho del Rosa."

"Yes, and I own the mortgage on it. What do I want of a ranch? Breen said it wasn't worth that much money, but that we—oh, damn Breen! He said we needed that much money, and that it would be as safe—what does he say? Have you seen Breen?"

Sohmes was panting as though he had been running.

"Breen doesn't know any more than I do. Only Wong Kee and Dell Harper knew—and they're both dead."

"Hijackers?" whispered Sohmes. "Did they get it?"

"Breen don't think so."

"Then who got it? The officers didn't, did they? Not the hijackers? Who is left? Have some of our own men double-crossed us? Maxwell, I'm going down to Gomez Springs. Never mind about the Border Patrol. This is my last trip down there, anyway; I'm through.

"Maybe," he grinned sourly, "I'll take this ranch and raise cows."

Maxwell said nothing. He followed Sohmes down to the patio, but they did not shake hands. Sohmes was too agitated to think of such a thing, and drove away without even a nod of his head. Maxwell watched them go, and they headed directly for Gomez Springs. Sohmes was not going to lose any time in talking with Breen.

And things were not going so well with Breen. Lobo Gomez wanted to raid the Maxwell ranch and run off their cattle. Lobo knew where he could sell the whole herd, and he had men enough to do the job, but Breen opposed the idea. Down in Breen's heart was the conviction that Maxwell had nothing to do with the missing diamonds.

He knew that the loss would break Maxwell, Sohmes would get the Rancho del Rosa, and he would be able to buy it from Sohmes pretty cheaply. He didn't want those cattle touched. He and Gomez had quarreled, and only the level-headed advice of Lee Duck stopped a gun fight. Gomez had gone away angry, swearing to do as he pleased, which he probably would.

Breen was half-drunk when Sohmes found him; in just the right mood to consider that he didn't owe Sohmes anything, and he wanted to know what in hell Sohmes was doing in Mexico. Sohmes told him, and he also told him of his conversation with Maxwell.

"And so you came down here to find out if it was true, eh?"

"Wouldn't I naturally be interested? I've lost ten thousand—"

"Oh, shut up! What's ten thousand dollars?"

"And I took a mortgage on that Maxwell ranch, didn't I? That money is all gone, too."

"What'll you sell that mortgage for right now?"

"Sell it? To you?"

"What do you care who you sell it to?"

"I'll sell it for what I paid."

"How long have you been crazy like this, Sohmes?"

"You think it isn't worth what I paid?"

"I know damn well it isn't. I told you at the time that it wasn't worth the money, but that we had to have it. You might be able to find a sucker to pay you that price, at that."

"Well, I'm in no hurry, Breen. If Maxwell can pay the interest, I'll let things ride. After seeing the place, I might keep it myself."

"Suit yourself. How about a little drink? What else did Maxwell tell you?"

"Nothing. I brought that mortgage along with me, to turn over to him if the diamonds were placed in my hands. I've got a cash buyer, I tell you."

"You'd turn that mortgage over, without any money changing hands?"

"Why not? I'd just deduct the price of the diamonds."

"Mm-m-m-m," thoughtfully. "Well, let's have a drink."

They went to the bar and had their drink, where Lee Duck joined them. Breen told Lee what Sohmes had told him, which was merely that

136

Sohmes had talked with Maxwell and found out about the missing diamonds.

"I found out something else," said Lee Duck, who talked both English and Spanish fluently. "The night Berg was knocked out and tied to that horse, only three of the Maxwell cowboys were in Sicomoro—Neeley, Eads, and Herrera. They were at the One Oak Cantina until midnight."

"That leaves Snow and that red-headed Davidson, eh?"

"They were not in Sicomoro."

"I'd like to make somebody a bet that Davidson is a Government spy."

"And working at the Maxwell ranch?" asked Sohmes anxiously.

"If I could get my hands on him for a few hours, I'd find out. I've got a settlement coming with that party."

"Better keep on this side of the line," advised Lee Duck.

"Do you suppose Maxwell told Davidson that he was coming down here to see me? If he didn't, how in the world would Davidson know where to look for him? Davidson is the man we need. He discovered the body of Dell Harper, and maybe he got the diamonds. But how to get him down here? I'll have a talk with Gomcz, and see what he suggests, if he isn't too sore at me to talk. Some day I'm going to shoot him full of holes."

"If he does not shoot you first, my friend,"

smiled the Chinaman. He turned to Sohmes, "Are you going to stay here for a while?"

"He's going out to spend the night at my rancho," said Breen quickly.

"That's all right," agreed Sohmes. "I'll send the boy back with the buggy."

They walked out and paid the Mexican, who started back for Sicomoro, while the two men went back to the cantina. They had a few more drinks. Sohmes was not a heavy drinker, and he drank more than usual. Breen had some hand-rolled cigarettes in a metal case, and offered them to Sohmes, who smoked one.

When Sohmes had consumed half of the cigarette, he looked at it curiously.

"What's in that cigarette, Breen?"

Breen laughed shortly. "Oh, just a little marahuana."

"Do you smoke that stuff all the time?"

"Quite a lot."

"Not for me." Sohmes ground the cigarette under his heel. "I wondered what was in it. I'd just as soon snuff coke."

"Don't you like the effect?"

"I do not."

"It calms your nerves."

"I suppose it does. Nerves you up for most anything. Do we eat here or out at your ranch?"

"Oh, we may as well eat out there. I'll send a boy out to saddle horses for us."

Breen took a supply of liquor along in a sack, which he tied to the saddle.

"Have to take something out to the boys," he explained, as they rode out of town. "They're a dry lot."

There was no road out to Breen's ranch, only a trail, which led in and out of the little valleys, skirting the mesquite thickets and along the dry-washes, where the desert smoke-trees flourished. Sohmes was in the lead, riding squattily in his saddle. Breen was close behind him, and as they crossed a dry-wash, where the hoofs of the horses cut deeply in the soft sand, Breen suddenly spurred in closer to Sohmes, and fired one shot from his revolver.

The diamond merchant slumped forward like a sack of meal, slid down past the shoulder of his startled horse, and went headlong into the sand. Breen jerked up his horse and looked at the inert figure. He sat there for several moments, his mouth twisted queerly, and then dismounted.

He dropped his reins and walked over to Sohmes. Breen was as cool over it all as though he was looking at anything rather than a man he had just shot. He lighted another cigarette and smoked thoughtfully for a while. Finally he grasped Sohmes under the arms and began carrying him down the wash. It was hot out there, and the perspiration poured from Breen's face.

Far down the wash he carried him, resting at intervals, finally dropping Sohmes behind a thicket of mesquite. Then he proceeded to search through Sohmes's pockets, until he found a thick billfold. A glance at the contents showed that Sohmes had been carrying an extraordinary lot of money with him.

"The fool!" grunted Breen. "As much as told me he had money along to pay for the diamonds. Fat-headed fool."

Breen went back to the horses, where he smoked again and debated over his next move. Finally he picked up the reins of the horse Sohmes had ridden, mounted his own horse, and rode for at least a mile up the wash, where he coolly shot the horse through the head, after he had removed the saddle, which he took farther up the wash and dumped into another mesquite thicket where no one would ever find it.

A little later he rode in at the ranch and gave the boys the liquor.

"We almost had company," he told them, laughing a little. "Sohmes, the diamond fence, came down to Gomez Springs, wondering where those diamonds had gone. He sent his rig back to Sicomoro, and was going to ride out here with me, but changed his mind and cut back to Sicomoro. He's sure mad about losing all that money.

"Tell the Chink to cook us some steaks, will

you, Mahan? And tell him I'll slice off his ears, if they're too well done."

"You didn't find out who slugged me, didja?" asked Berg. His head was still too sore to wear a hat.

Breen laughed softly. "Lee Duck checked up on things, probably with a Chink in Sicomoro, and found out that Johnny Snow and the redhead were the only boys from Maxwell's place who were not in Sicomoro that night. They were the ones who hit you, Berg."

"That's fine," growled Berg. "I'll collect me a red scalp."

Silent grinned widely, and Berg noticed it.

"You think I won't?" he asked belligerently.

"I think you'll try," replied Silent. "It seems to me that the redhead is pretty much of a salty gent. He smoked up Joe Pico, who you boys claim to be somethin' whatever with a gun. He runs a sandy on our friend Breen, and then he puts yore head out of commission and trades yuh for another party. That scalp might cost yuh somethin', Berg."

"He never ran any sandy on me," growled Breen. "I'd look fine startin' a gun battle in Maxwell's patio. And no matter what he's done, it's nothing for you to swell up about. You're paid to do what you're told."

Silent shoved his hands deep in his pockets. He wanted to go over and tie Breen in a knot.

Perhaps Breen realized this, because he said:

"There's no question about the redhead being a tough hombre, as far as that goes, Slade. They tell me Joe Pico had his hand on his gun, and the redhead beat him to the draw. That's speed."

Slade nodded and turned away. He wanted to tell that he could take Brick and whip the whole bunch of them, but he knew better. His immediate future was worth more to him than idle boasts.

After Breen went in the house, Eddy walked down to the corral with Silent, while they put up Breen's horse.

"Breen gits under yore hide, too, don't he?" said Eddy. "He shore gits under mine."

"Kinda hauled in his horns, didn't he?"

"Don't never figure him thataway, pardner. He can't afford to have any trouble with us, because he don't jist figure how we stand. We're all in the same boat, yuh see, and we *might* stick together—against him. He's the boss, as long as we'll be bossed. But don't trust him too far. He's a tequila hound, and he mixes marahuana with his tobacco. It's a fine combination, if yuh want to murder somebody."

"Oh, yea-a-ah," softly. It was the first time Silent knew that Breen smoked the weed. He thought it over for a few minutes, while Eddy gave the horse a feed of oats.

"Was you workin' for Breen six months ago?" he asked.

"Jist about. I was down in Chihuahua for a while, and then I worked my way up here. No, it wasn't quite that long ago. Breen wasn't here at that time, but he came along, and I got acquainted with him."

"Where had he been?" asked Silent. "He's been down here a long time."

"Oh, he was up around Frisco, I reckon. I heard him talk about it. Why?"

"Oh, I jist wondered if I hadn't seen him somewhere before."

"How did you ever git in with him, Slade?"

Silent laughed softly. "Oh, I met him in Gomez Springs. He asked me if my name was Slade, and I told him it was. He had me scared for a minute, even if I was in Mexico. Then he told me that he had seen a reward notice at the sheriff's office in Sicomoro. He said he often went there and kinda checked over on them kinda things. It shore scared me. I didn't realize that a reward notice would come this far.

"But I rode to Sicomoro with him later on. He said I was perfectly safe, because the sheriff probably hadn't never read the notice, because it happened away up in Montana. But I'm not goin' back there again. They was all fixed to hang me."

"Pleasant thought," grinned Eddy. "But yo're all right, as long as yuh stay down here. The Mexicans ain't goin' to worry about us. They've got too much trouble of their own to bother about a few Americans who might be in bad with their own country.

"Breen says that as soon as he's made plenty money down here, he's goin' to retire, buy a home in California and be a gentleman. He'll make the money, and he'll probably buy the home, but I'll be damned if he'll ever be a gentleman. If the truth was known, he'd be hung higher'n a kite the first time he went across the line. If you hadn't been with him all that day, I'd bet that he killed Dell Harper and stole the diamonds, and then framed up on Wong Kee. Oh, he's plenty capable of it, Slade."

"I reckon that's right," sighed Silent. "I kinda look for him and Lobo Gomez to lock horns any old time. If it hadn't been for the Chinaman, they'd have shot it out the last time. Lobo's got his mind fixed to steal them cows, and Breen better let him go ahead. It would save trouble."

Eddy laughed, as he tossed the feed bucket aside.

"I'll tell yuh somethin', Slade: Breen's afraid of the redhead. He's mad every time anybody mentions redheads. And that redhead better look out, because if Breen ever gets him across the line—good-bye, redhead."

"He'd shore make a try at it," agreed Silent wearily. "Let's go up and get some of that liquor, before that gang lap it all up."

CHAPTER IX

THE PICOS DISCUSS DELL HARPER

JOE PICO was able to sit up again, and would be out in a few days. The wound had healed well, but his shoulder was stiff and very sore. He sat there in bed and scowled at Al and Bill Abelardo, who were sprawled in chairs near him, perfectly sober, for a wonder. Edward Pico sat on the foot of the bed, smoking a long, black cigar.

"Theese radhad ees ver' bad," said Al Abelardo monotonously. "He's tie me and Beel to a—"

"Oh, shut up!" snapped Joe. "You never know when to quit talkin'. I wish he had tied the rope around your damn necks. You've told that story twenty times."

Ed Pico chuckled. Perhaps he had a sense of humor. He turned to Joe, shifted the cigar in his mouth for a moment, and then turned to Al and Bill.

"Vamos," he said.

"Si," nodded Al, and they filed out together. Ed Pico waited until they shut the door before he turned to Joe.

"Tell me what happened the day you got shot."

Joe blinked quickly. "I think you have heard," he replied in Spanish.

"What happened before that?"

"Oh!" softly. "What do you know?"

"I know you killed Harper."

Joe grimaced and reached for a glass of water on a little table. He gulped it down, and, his hand shook a little, as he put it back.

"What did Harper have with him, Joe?"

"Nothing."

"Are you sure?"

"I didn't search him."

Ed Pico scowled at Joe, who twisted uneasily. "Don't lie to me."

"Why would I search him?"

"Why did you kill him?"

"He reached for his gun."

"Oh, he did, did he? You don't tell me anything. Tell me what happened."

"I was in Gomez Springs that day, but I didn't see Harper. When I came back I overtook him this side of the Rancho del Rosa. I don't think he came by road, but through the hill on the east side. I know he was down in Gomez Springs that day, because Wong Hop told me he was the other day, when he was down to see me. Wong Hop don't know I shot him. I met Harper, as I have said. You know we have never been friends, and I had been drinking. I jerked up my horse, intending to speak with him, and he reached for his gun. That was all.

"I came to town and met that infernal redhead.

You have heard the rest. But I did not search Harper. Why do you ask me if I did?"

Ed Pico rubbed his chin thoughtfully, as he puffed on his cigar.

"I have heard," he said slowly, "that Harper carried a million dollars' worth of diamonds with him that day, and they are gone."

"Madre de Dios!" Joe sat up like a mechanical toy, his jaw sagging. He sank limply back against the pillow, staring at his brother.

"And I failed to look for them!"

"So it seems."

"Since when did Dell Harper begin smuggling?"

Ed Pico laughed shortly, but shook his head.

"Who knows? A Chinaman, who works for Lee Duck, tells many things to Wong Hop; but he does not tell it all, because he is afraid of Lee Duck. But it is enough for our use."

"Is Maxwell working with Breen?"

"That we do not know. Keep your mouth shut. No one suspects you of killing Harper. Now, what about these fool cousins of ours? They got drunk and went down to the Casa del Rosa to avenge you. Neither of them knows exactly what happened, except that no men were there, until several came back and discovered them. Al says a dozen men came; Bill says he counted thirty. But of course, neither of them can count very well. The redhead came back, they say, and attempted to hang them, but did not finish the job."

Joe laughed shortly and lighted a cigarette.

"The fools mean well, I suppose. Give them a little more time, and they will both be hung. When I am well again, we will do some more work."

"My advice will be for you to forget this redhead."

"And I may accept that advice. The man has the luck of the devil, and shoots well. I swear I did not see him draw his gun. If he keeps out of my way, the incident is closed. I have need of my own skin. But who got the diamonds?"

"That is for us to discover. The redhead found Harper's body."

"I have heard that. Suppose he has the diamonds?"

"Would he stay down here, if he had that many diamonds?"

"You make my head ache, brother. A million dollars' worth!"

"More or less. Such things are always exaggerated."

"It does not require many diamonds to be worth a million. I spent five hundred for a measly ring for a girl in the Gomez cantina, and she ran away with a goat-herder from Chihuahua. I know what diamonds are worth. Some day I shall find that goat-herder and cut off his ears."

"Look North for her," said Edward coldly. "Wong Hop told me the other day that both the girl and the goat-herder from Chihuahua were not from Chihuahua at all, but spies of this Government. They had enough information to send several men to a Federal prison, but they were discovered and made their escape. That was why Scotty McKee sold out and left here so quickly; they had information, he thought, which might put him in prison. That was one of the reasons he left so quickly, and made me a bargain price on the One Oak Cantina."

"And I gave a five-hundred-dollar diamond to a spy?"

"That is what Wong Hop told me. He is more than a year late on his information, but it did not affect us."

"That is not true. I spent five hundred—"

"It was a small price, Joe. If that woman had stayed, you might have told her where you got the five hundred."

"That is true," thankfully. "A man is sometimes a fool."

"Always a fool, where women are concerned. Let it be a lesson."

"I shall buy no more diamonds. I learn easily."

Edward Pico went back about his business of running cantinas, until the hijacking business might pick up a little. It had been bad lately. The energies and the ready cash of the smugglers had been employed in the diamond business, which seemed to have failed. Edward Pico had seen

Sohmes, the diamond merchant, in Sicomoro that day. He knew who Sohmes was, and he guessed rightly that Sohmes was down there to find out more about the missing diamonds.

Edward Pico was the level-headed member of his gang. Joe was hot-headed, the Abelardo brothers plain ignorant. But the Abelardos were handy in a fight, and they didn't ask for any big split of the profits. Anyway, the money was kept in the family. It was a dangerous game, hijacking.

That same afternoon Brick and Johnny rode in south of Sicomoro. Slim wasn't satisfied with the count of the cattle they had driven to the north range, and he wanted Johnny and Brick to take another look. Slim wasn't aware of the fact that many of the Maxwell Diamond M brand had gone to feed hungry mouths across the line.

Brick carried a thirty-thirty Winchester on his saddle and a pocket full of cartridges. They combed the brushy draws, until they were near the old Pico rancho, southwest of Sicomoro, but did not find any stock belonging to the Diamond M.

"I reckon Slim was all wrong," said Johnny. "Mebby a lot of cows drifted north ahead of our little round-up."

"That's probably the reason," agreed Brick, as they dismounted on a rocky pinnacle and sat down in the shade to roll a smoke.

"That's the old Pico rancho over there," said

Johnny, pointing out a huddle of old adobe buildings, southwest of where they sat. "Used to be a real cow-ranch, I understand, but the Pico outfit played out. All the old families are playin' out down here. There won't be a Maxwell left, after the old man dies."

"And you'll marry Marie," smiled Brick, "and then—"

"Go ahead and have yore fit," grunted Johnny. "I've got about as much chance to marry her as I have of bein' President of Mexico."

"She seems like a real sensible girl."

"That's the worst of it."

"Mm-m-m-m," mumbled Brick, his eyes fixed on a point just south of the old Pico ranch buildings, where a long brushy swale extended southward. The sun was getting low along the western hills, and part of this swale was shadowed.

"Whatcha see?" asked Johnny. Brick got to his feet leaning against a shaft of granite, his hat pulled low over his eyes.

"I saw somethin' movin' over there. There it is again! It's cattle and men. Look just below that low break. See 'em?"

Johnny was on his feet now, straining his eyes against the low sun.

"I saw 'em, Brick! The sun glinted on somethin'. Dang it, I get that sun in my eyes and I can't see anythin'."

They ran to their horses and mounted swiftly.

"Sun flashin' on metal," grunted Brick. "Them Mexicans wear a lot of silver and—I see 'em again. They're—they've got some cows ahead of 'em. It's Mexicans, pardner. C'mon."

Brick swung his horse down along the pinnacle, with Johnny riding close in behind them. To the right of them was a dry wash, with steep, rocky banks; no chance for them to cross. The ridge they were on was rocky, brushy, forcing them to detour widely. It was not over a half-mile to the Border.

Brick tried to lead the way and keep off the crest of the ridge, but found himself blocked by a quarry-like cut, and they were obliged to scramble back to the sky-line. They could see the Mexicans now. There were at least eight of them, bunched together, and ahead of them were six beef steers, heading south. The men were about four hundred yards from Brick and Johnny, traveling almost parallel.

But the Mexicans had the advantage, as ahead of them was only a gentle slope to the Border, while Brick and Johnny were still on that ridge, with plenty of rough going ahead of them.

"They see us!" exclaimed Johnny, as the riders suddenly separated. Brick was drawing out his rifle, adjusting the sights, when a bullet hit a rock above them, and went whining off across the hills.

Johnny swore feelingly. The cattle had stopped and were swinging around, when two of the riders went galloping down to turn them back. The others were well separated, but moving toward the Border. Brick dismounted and rested his rifle across a rock. The light was bad, as he was shooting almost against the sun, which was nearly down.

His first shot struck in the sand just short of a rider, and caused that worthy to duck low and spur his horse to an awkward gallop.

"Fifty yards more," said Brick, setting the peep sight carefully.

This time he aimed at one of the riders, who had drawn up behind a screen of mesquite and was evidently getting ready for a shot at the two cowboys.

The thirty-thirty whanged again, and Johnny exploded joyfully, when the horse went down and the rider went sprawling. He regained his feet and went hippety-hopping down that slope, jumping into the air like a startled jack rabbit, when Brick's next bullet struck a rock just in front of him, sending up a white puff of stone-dust.

Brick stuffed more shells through the loading-gate of his rifle and looked for another victim. The Mexicans were not doing any more shooting. The two riders had turned the cattle and were galloping them down across that desert flat, dust trailing up behind them.

The other riders were hugging the brush, keeping out of sight.

"They're delayin' us, until them two jiggers get the beef across the line," wailed Johnny.

And he was right. The sun went down behind the peaks, and the two riders were well down to the Border, their dust alone visible to Brick and Johnny. Night comes quickly after the sunset in the Southwest. Brick knew that there would be no chance to stop the raiders, who could get across the Border before he and Johnny could get off that rough ridge.

Somewhere down in that dark tangle of brush were the other riders, waiting for darkness, content to stay there until this Americano vaquero could not see to shoot at them. He had killed one horse, and they didn't want to spare another.

"Aw, rats!" snorted Brick at last. "They've got us stuck, and they know it. But I've got a lotta shells left, and I'm shore goin' to make 'em keep their heads down. Listen for a yelp."

He settled down, placed a handful of cartridges on the rock beside him, and proceeded to spray lead all over the approximate location of the raiders, while the darkening hills echoed back the reports of the rifle. He saved a magazine full of shells, shoved the rifle back in the scabbard, and mounted his horse.

"That was actin' like a spoiled kid," he told

Johnny disgustedly. "I do the craziest things. Mebby it's my red head."

"Well, I'll betcha you had them rustlers huggin' the dirt."

"What good does that do? I'm wonderin' where they take the beef?"

"Gomez Springs, I reckon. Mebby they take 'em to Breen's rancho. He's got a place down there. Had six animals, didn't they?"

"I think so. That'll keep 'em eatin' for a few days. Mebby we better not tell Slim about this, Johnny. We'll tell Maxwell, and if he says it's all right, we'll tell Slim."

"This will shore worry Maxwell. When they start raidin' across—look out for trouble. Breen is behind all this, you can bet on that. Looks as though they were merely takin' enough to eat, but it was prob'ly because we cleaned out this end of the ranch. They'll come back again."

"Well, when they do," grinned Brick, "I hope I have plenty shells and the sun to my back. Anyway, we made two of 'em ride double."

But Brick did better than he thought. About two hours after Brick and Johnny had ridden off that pinnacle, Lobo Gomez and his six men rode in at Breen's ranch. One of the men was so badly hurt that he was tied to his horse, one man was without any horse, and Lobo Gomez was a sight to behold.

His left eye was only a purple puff, with hardly

even a fold to show where his eye might be, and his right cheek was badly cut and swollen. They brought six of Maxwell's beef steers, which they put in the corral.

Gomez was almost frying with rage, as he told Breen what had happened. Breen was two-thirds drunk, and Lobo Gomez's tale of woe amused him. The big bandit told of how he and his men went to raid the range across the line, only to find that the cattle had been moved.

They found six head near the old Pico ranch, and were heading for the Border when the two cowboys discovered them. Gomez explained how four of them went under cover, after one horse had been killed, and two of his men had gone on after the six beeves.

"And then," he said painfully, "we watched closely. I had a pair of binoculars, with which I could see plainly. I saw that redhead. He was without his hat, which was on the rock beside him. None of us were in sight, but he began shooting. I heard Felipe cry out. Bullets were flying through the brush. Then I looked again, and something struck me with terrific force. Later I discovered that a bullet had struck my binoculars, driving them into my eye and cutting my cheek. That man is a devil, I tell you."

"You better go to town and have a doctor for you and Felipe," said Breen. "You paid well for six steers."

"The fool shot at nothing, I tell you!"

"You look it, Lobo," grinned Breen.

Lobo glowered with his one good eye, which was also beginning to assume a purple shade from the swelling on his cheek.

"I told you to let those cattle alone," reminded Breen.

"Who are you to tell me what to do? Mejico would be better off without you drunken gringoes."

"Certainly," agreed Breen. "You'd be running around without shoes, eating tortillas and frijoles, and without a peso to your name. Bah! Your father was a goat-herder and your mother was a Yaqui squaw. I've made you more money in a year than the Gomez family ever saw; and I'll make you more money, but you've got to obey orders."

Gomez drank deeply of tequila and considered Breen's statement. It was very true, even to the ancestry. The potent liquor warmed his veins and took some of the sting from his injuries.

"You better take Felipe to town," said Breen.

"Yes," agreed Gomez.

"And when you bring me the redhead, I shall give you a thousand pesos."

Lobo Gomez grinned widely. This was something different. Breen had always warned him against any operations across the Border, and now he was offering real money for the redhead.

"Have the money counted for me," he boasted, drinking again. "It is a good price. Ho! Juan! See that Felipe is securely tied to his horse; we are going to Gomez Springs."

He bowed to Breen, struck his shoulder against the side of the door, as he went out, following his men.

"Ignorant pig!" snorted Breen, speaking in English. "As soon as his eyes are normal again, he'll go raiding across the line. Who cares? He will either bring me the redhead or leave his own carcass to rot on American soil."

"A raid might cause a lot of merry hell along the border," said Mahan.

"Certainly. But what's the difference? Our game is ruined. Unless I am mistaken, this redhead is a Government spy. If it was he who took Maxwell back from Gomez Springs, he knows too much. Through some leak, the Border Patrol knew about those diamonds, and the redhead came to work for Maxwell. They suspect Maxwell. Perhaps it is more than a suspicion.

"I believe there are spies in Gomez City; spies for the Government and spies for the hijackers. Let me get my hands on that redhead, and we'll know the truth. I'll burn the soles off his bare feet. Damn him, he'll be ready to talk before I finish with him."

Breen laughed drunkenly and helped himself to more liquor, while Silent humped against the

158

wall, wondering how he might get word to Brick. Silent was disgusted with Breen, disgusted with everything down in that country. He wanted to get away from there; but there was no place to go, unless he headed south.

"How will Lobo ever get his hands on the redhead?" asked Mahan, who had little faith in Gomez's ability.

"His methods don't worry me," laughed Breen. "He'll probably take a lot of half-starved peons, arm them with a lot of antique rifles, and take him by force. A thousand pesos means a lot to Gomez."

"I'll be damned if I like the idea," growled Mahan.

"*You* don't, eh? Well, what do you care what happens? They'd hang you, if you went across the line."

"You don't need to tell me that, Breen. But to pay a damn half-breed Yaqui to raid white people!"

"I'm not payin' him to raid anybody. I want that redhead. What he does, while he gets me that redhead, is none of my affairs."

"If I was you, I'd let that redhead alone," said Silent. "He'll be bad medicine to you, Breen. Mebby redheads are yore jinx. He's shore throwed a lot of monkey-wrenches into yore machinery since he showed up in this country; and I've got a hunch that if you fool with him much more he'll hand you a harp."

159

Breen laughed harshly, as though amused.

"Listen to the oracle," he said. "Do you read palms, or merely tell the past, present, and future from a hunch?"

"Sometimes I read palms."

"The hell you do! Read mine, will you?"

Breen held out his hand toward Silent, who got slowly up from his haunches and came across the room. Breen didn't expect this. His hand was rather unsteady, as Silent looked down at it, his eyes half-shut, as though in concentration.

"Well, what do you see?" growled Breen.

Silent lifted his head and looked at Breen.

"Do yuh want me to tell out loud what I see?" he asked softly.

Breen jerked his hand back, looking at it curiously. He had not washed since coming to the ranch, and there was a smear of blood across the heel of his hand. But Silent couldn't know what happened on the trail. Breen rubbed his hand on his knee, his bloodshot eyes fixed on the big cowboy.

"You lie!" he said thickly. "You can't read palms."

Silent laughed shortly and turned away.

"I can read 'em all right, if you'd like to listen," he said.

But Breen didn't want to listen. He was afraid.

"Read mine," laughed Eddy. Silent shook his head.

"You probably never killed a friend, Eddy."

"Damn you!" Breen jumped to his feet, but halted short. Silent was leaning forward, a huge bulk in the yellow light of the lamp, his right hand tensed, fingers spread wide over the butt of his Colt. For several moments neither of them moved. Then Breen laughed gratingly and sank back in his chair.

"Oh, all right," he said weakly. "Bring in some more of that tequila, Berg. Let's all have a big drink before we go to bed. No use of us quarreling. We've got enough trouble, without fighting among ourselves."

"That's right," agreed Mahan hastily. "Too damn much trouble. It's all right for you to get drunk out here, Breen; but you ought to keep sober in town. You talk too much when you're drunk, and if that fat-headed Lobo ever does raid across the line, and there's any suspicion that you paid him to do it, you'll have the Mexican soldiers on yore trail too damn quick. This Government is tryin' to be friendly with the States, and they'd stand you against a blank wall too damn quick, if they thought you started trouble for them."

"I'll run my own business."

"Go ahead, and see if I mourn at yore grave."

"Perhaps you forget that I am paying you for your work. I am the boss of this rancho, Mahan."

"Boss! We're workin' for yuh, Breen; but you

don't own this rancho any more than we do. You'd look well bossin' us, if we didn't want to be bossed. Yo're as yaller as the sunflowers down along the dry-wash. Boss! You better stick to smugglin'."

Breen shut his lips tightly and scowled at the tequila bottle. There was a lot of truth in what Mahan said. He was yellow, and he knew it. He had been foolish enough to imagine that he dominated these men, and now he knew they detested him. But he would play possum, until he was through with their services.

"I think I'll go back to Gomez Springs," he said heavily. "Will one of you boys saddle my horse?"

Mahan grinned. It was a different tone of voice now.

"I'll tell Gomez to merely get me the redhead," continued Breen. "I think it might be dangerous for him to attempt a raid."

"Now, yo're showin' some sense," said Mahan. "It would be."

CHAPTER X

BRICK MAKES A DISCOVERY

THAT night Brick had a talk with Maxwell and told him about the rustlers. Maxwell did not seem surprised.

"I'm sure they have been doing that for a long time," he said. "It was Lobo Gomez and his gang, but I'm afraid that the only reason they didn't take more cattle was because we had shifted the herd to the north ranges. It is, I think, their first move at retaliation."

Maxwell told Brick about Sohmes being at the rancho.

"I don't think Breen will ever dare to come here," said Maxwell. "He has always been free to go back and forth, although I happen to know the Border Patrol are certain he is a smuggler. He knows I am through with him and his profession, if you can call it that. I trusted Breen. I have always been a gambler, Davidson—an unlucky gambler, and when Breen showed me a chance to put the Rancho del Rosa on its feet, I took the chance."

"Well, it wasn't a piker bet," smiled Brick.

He found Marie and Juanita on the patio veranda, and sat down on the steps with them. Over in the bunk-house, Johnny Snow was trying to play the guitar while Leo sang a Spanish love song. Neither of them was in tune. Brick remembered hearing Juanita sing the same song. He could see her, seated at the old piano in their old ranch-house in Sun Dog, singing that song, while Silent sat on the edge of a chair, twisting his sombrero in his hands.

He looked at her now, and she was resting her chin on her hands, her face in the moonlight. Something glistened suspiciously like a tear on her cheek.

"Juanita told me—about you, Brick," said Marie softly.

"About me?" Brick looked up quickly.

"I knew you had met before. That day in Sicomoro—when she came."

"Oh!" said Brick softly. "It wasn't so good to hear."

"You saved a friend."

"I gave him a chance."

"And threw away your chances," said Juanita. "I had to tell her, Brick. She knew we had met before. I told her about you and Silent."

"Thasall right; I'm not flyin' any false colors. I'm even usin' my own name down here."

"I told her all about my father's troubles," said Marie.

"Dog-gone! Well, I guess women can't help tellin' things. Let one of 'em get a secret, and they ache all over until they can tell it to somebody."

"You're not mad, are you?" asked Juanita quickly.

"No-o-o; not even surprised."

"You don't like women, do you?" asked Marie.

"You make a statement and ask a question at the same time," grinned Brick. "Which one are yuh goin' to use?"

"Do you?"

"Hm-m-m! Then you ain't sure, eh? Do I? I dunno. Mebby I do, and I'm jist a little cautious. Mebby I'm like Soapy Caswell. He said that a little women is like a little liquor—it exhilarates yuh; but too much women is like too much whisky—it made his head ache."

"Suppose we said the same about men?" queried Marie.

"That'd suit me. I don't know what yuh can see about the critters at all. If any woman ever said she loved me, I'd buy her a sack of nuts and tell her to pick a tall tree and enjoy herself."

While they were laughing, Johnny Snow came across the patio from the bunk-house and joined them.

"Now, yuh take Johnny, for instance," said Brick. "He loves women. He can't no more help bein' in love than he can stop breathin'. It's jist his nature. He's in love with a girl down in this country, but he won't tell what her name is."

"Brick, you dern idiot!" breathed Johnny, ready to stampede.

"Who is she, Johnny?" asked Marie.

"Oh, the danged idiot," wailed Johnny. "I ain't in love with no girl. I mean that no girl—oh, I don't know what I mean."

"Folks in love never do," said Brick. "Love's a funny thing, don'tcha know it? Makes yuh think with a reverse-English. Johnny's been in love a long time. Puts his saddle on backwards and gets his boots on the wrong feet."

"I never did! Don'tcha believe him. Bein' in love—"

"He admits it. Ain't it wonderful?"

"I hope to die if I don't massacree yuh, Brick Davidson."

"Who is the girl, Johnny?" asked Marie again. "Do I know her?"

"No, that ain't fair," interrupted Brick. "Yo're shootin' both barrels at him, Marie."

Johnny flinched.

"One barrel was enough," he said.

"Oh, I was so sorry about that, Johnny," said Marie.

"Thasall right. It was the only time I ever seen Brick busy enough to mind his own dang business."

"My shoulder is still sore," said Marie, trying hard to keep from laughing.

"I can laugh now," said Juanita, "but it wasn't funny at the time. There was Marie, running up the stairs, with one of those men running after her, and he fell just at the bottom of the steps, firing his gun. He had the queerest expression on his face, when he got up. And when I had presence of mind enough left to warn them that she would get the shotgun, they both tried to go out through the doorway together.

"I don't know just why I did it, but I picked up that bottle and threw it toward them as hard as I could. I saw it strike the fat one on the head, and I wondered if I had killed him."

"No such luck," laughed Johnny. "The Abelardos have hard heads."

"And I thought they were mounting their horses in the patio; so I put the muzzle of that gun through the open window, and fired. It never entered my head that it might be somebody else out there."

"It's a good thing it didn't enter Johnny's head," laughed Brick.

"I suppose I'll never hear the last of that," sighed Marie.

"Well, I never mentioned it," said Johnny quickly. "That danged redhead had to rake it up again."

They talked for a few minutes longer, then Marie excused herself. Johnny didn't stay long after Marie left, and in a few minutes they could hear him strumming on the guitar.

"Who is his girl?" asked Juanita.

"I dunno," laughed Brick. "Mebby it's you or Marie."

"Marie thinks a lot of Johnny."

"Shore thing?"

"Why not?"

"I'm not goin' to argue with yuh. He's a nice kid."

"Are you sorry I told her who you are, Brick?"

"It didn't make any difference."

"Brick," softly, "do you know where Silent Slade is?"

"Right now, I couldn't tell yuh. As I said before, I've never heard from him since the night he left Marlin City."

"You've talked with him?"

"Not a word."

Juanita sighed deeply and got to her feet.

"I'm sorry," said Brick. "If he was down in this country, he'd be afraid to come across the line."

"You mean—he is? Brick, don't lie to me."

"I don't know. Yuh see, I'm afraid to go across and look."

"You—afraid?"

"I shore am. Mebby we'll find him some day."

Juanita shook her head. "I'm not going to stay here. Marie told me all their troubles, and I feel that it is an imposition on my part to stay here. Don't you know that Mr. Maxwell has lost everything?"

"Yeah, he got into a mess all right. But don't go yet. Stick around and see the fireworks."

"What fireworks?"

"Oh, I was just talkin'. But don't go for a few days. Anythin' can happen in an hour."

"Aren't you afraid to stay here, Brick?"

"I shore am. No jokin'. I'm settin' on a stick of dynamite, and I know it. But I'm goin' to stick, like a danged fool. I reckon it's my red hair."

The following morning Brick and Johnny rode back through the south range, but this time they both carried rifles. Slim had told them to comb the country beyond Sicomoro, but when they reached the place where they had done their shooting the evening before, Brick decided to take a look at the dead horse.

They had no difficulty in finding the animal. The saddle had been removed and taken away. The brand was from a horse outfit in Sonora. Brick went further down in the little wash, where he had last seen the raiders, and here he found a blood-soaked handkerchief and the smashed binoculars.

He took them back to the horses and showed them to Johnny.

"I shore popped one of them jiggers," he declared. "If he was lookin' through them glasses, I'll bet I spoiled the scenery for him."

"What a look he got!" exploded Johnny, examining the glasses. "Let me tell yuh, pardner, no common Mex ever owned them glasses."

"Well, they're ruined now," grinned Brick. He

169

sat there and looked down across the border for a while, while Johnny fussed with the glasses.

"Let's trail them steers," suggested Brick. "We might find out somethin'."

"Find out how it seems to be backed against a blank wall. You don't seem to realize that Mexico is danged bad medicine for me and you."

"I know; but couldn't we trail a little ways? We've both got guns."

"You knew danged well I'd go with yuh," grinned Johnny. "We'll find that the steers went to Gomez Springs, I suppose."

"And we won't follow them that far. It would be too much like walkin' into a quicksand, as long as our friend Breen is high-gun down there."

They picked up the trail of the steers and the riders. Few cattle had ever been taken across at that point, and the tracks were plain. They kept a close watch, but there was no danger of an ambush, unless somebody saw them coming.

The trail led southeast, heading directly for Gomez Springs, and the two boys were about to turn back, when the trail turned abruptly to the southwest, following along a dry wash.

"They're cuttin' back toward Breen's ranch," said Johnny. "I'll bet we strike the trail in a little while."

"We'll soon find out."

The brush was fairly thick along there, but the hills to the west were fairly open. Johnny was

170

just a little nervous. He wasn't sure where the Breen ranch was located, and he knew that Breen had a number of riders employed.

"You keep on that trail," he told Brick. "I'll hit for higher ground, where I can watch ahead."

Brick was willing; so he waited until Johnny was on the side of a hill, and they traveled parallel. The trail twisted and turned, following the main part of the wash, avoiding the thickets of mesquite, sage and smoke-trees, which grew in profusion along this particular wash.

At one point Brick swung his horse out of the heavy sand and was riding along higher ground toward a mesquite thicket, when he saw something which caused him to stop quickly. Not over twenty feet away, lying against the tangle of the thicket, was the body of a man.

It was Sohmes, the diamond fence, lying where Breen had left him, knowing that there was hardly one chance in a thousand of any one ever finding the body. Brick dismounted quickly and looked the man over. Beside the body was a notebook, a couple of envelopes, bearing the name of Hubert Sohmes.

"Murdered and robbed," decided Brick quickly, as he examined the notebook and letters.

The notebook merely contained some addresses, and the letters were from wholesale diamond merchants. The pockets of the coat were empty. An expensive watch had been left in

171

his vest, and on a finger was a large diamond ring.

Brick turned the body over and in a hip-pocket he found a legal appearing document, folded square to fit the pocket. It was the mortgage on the Rancho del Rosa. Brick took a deep breath as he looked it over. Brick had been familiar with all kinds of legal papers, and the first thing he looked for was the filing number, which he did not find. To all appearances the mortgage had never been filed.

He put the paper in his pocket, mounted his horse and hurried up the wash, trying to see where Johnny had gone. Suddenly he almost ran into several horsemen, who were crossing the wash, making too much noise to have heard him. There were five of them, and in the center of the single-file rode Silent Slade. The Breen outfit were going to town.

Brick stayed behind the screen of mesquite, until the riders were far across the dry-wash, before he ventured out. There was the deeply cut trail from Gomez Springs to the Breen rancho, and there were the tracks of the steers, which had turned into the trail, heading west.

Brick rode along this trail, wondering where Johnny was, when he came out from behind the brush and joined him.

"By golly, I was scared," said Johnny. "I seen them five fellers, but they were too close for me to do anythin'. I shore was scared that you'd run right into 'em."

Brick told him of finding the dead man, and they rode back together. Johnny had never seen Sohmes, and he wasn't very fond of dead men, anyway. Brick's examination showed that Sohmes had been shot in the back of the head, killing him instantly. Another search of his pockets revealed nothing more than a bunch of keys and a few cents in change.

Brick removed the watch, which was a small platinum affair, set with diamonds. Brick realized that it was a very expensive timepiece.

"Mebby we can send it back to his relatives," he said.

"You ain't intendin' to take the body back with us, are yuh?"

"Not a chance. We'll bury him the best we can, and let it go at that."

They had nothing to dig with; so they laid the body in a depression and covered it with stones from the wash. At least these would keep the buzzards and coyotes from consuming it. Brick marked the spot with a monument of stones some distance away, and then they mounted and rode back to the trail.

"What's on yore mind now?" asked Johnny.

"I've got a hunch that the Breen rancho is deserted. Let's ride over and take a look at it."

"My Gawd, you shore ain't got no brains, Brick!"

"I know it; but I'm perfectly happy."

"And I'm jist as crazy as you are, because I'm goin' with yuh."

And the two self-confessed idiots grinned at each other, as they headed toward the Breen rancho.

CHAPTER XI

GOMEZ GETS HIS ORDERS

WHEN Jim Breen left the rancho the night before it was the first time in his life he admitted to himself that things were beginning to break against him. There was no remorse in his heart over the murder of Sohmes, no fear of the consequences. And, according to his standards, he had been well paid for that single bullet.

Breen had been well raised, well educated. His father had been a prosperous Indiana farmer, who died before Jim became of age. But this made little difference to Jim, who was sojourning in Guatemala, a fugitive from Indiana justice for the killing of a farm hand over a fancied insult to a girl. It was probably Jim's only act in defense of virtue, and he often smiled over the incident.

He worked his way up through Mexico and eventually came to Sicomoro with plenty of money, which he invested in horses. It was five years after the killing in Indiana, and Breen felt safe again. For nearly five years he raised horses, during which time he gained the confidence of Robert Maxwell, who also loved horses.

But the horses did not pay heavy enough dividends; so he sold out, took his earnings and invested in Gomez Springs. He had a keen knowledge of that twenty miles of almost unprotected Border, and all he needed was some one on the American side to take care of what might be sent across, and another man or men to dispose of the stuff.

It was natural that he should take Lobo Gomez in with him. Gomez had an idea that he owned the town, and Breen couldn't afford to buck any such ideas. He felt that he could dispose of Gomez at any time. Reverses and double-dealings almost broke Breen, but he managed to survive, and later made his alliance with Maxwell, which he considered his master stroke, and also engaged the keen wits of Wong Kee to outwit the Border Patrol, as well as the hijackers.

But when he rode away from the rancho, he realized that he was all through. Maxwell would be against him now; Wong Kee dead. It had taken him a long time to make a business connection with Sohmes, and now that was broken. And strangely enough, he blamed it all on Brick Davidson. Things had been working smoothly until that redhead appeared. Why, he was even going to marry Marie Maxwell.

Strangely enough, he hadn't thought much about that. There had been so many other things to distract him. But he had plenty of money now. The murder of Sohmes would never be marked against him. And what if it was? There was no law in Gomez Springs. Sohmes was down there on his own responsibility.

He would sell out his interests in Gomez Springs and go south; perhaps to South America. No, he wouldn't do that. He was a big toad in a small puddle. In spite of Lobo Gomez, Breen owned Gomez Springs. If it came to a show-down, he would kill Gomez. That might be a good idea, he thought.

He would surely kill Lobo; and then he would kill the redhead. Perhaps he would kill the redhead first. Anyway, that was settled. Then he would build himself a wonderful home on the slope above Gomez Springs, and rule the town from his castle. And if the Mexican Government made an investigation, he would see that the people paid a fair tax, which they had never done before. And the big cantina could afford a tax.

Having settled everything in his unsettled mind, he arrived at Gomez Springs. He found Lee Duck, who told him that Gomez had arrived totally blind, and had been taken to a Mexican doctor for treatment. The Chinaman was a little amused, when Breen told him what happened to Gomez.

"Did Sohmes come back with you?" asked Lee Duck.

"He didn't go with me," growled Breen. "Decided to go back across the line. He will do no more business with us."

The Chinaman nodded thoughtfully. Then—

"He has the mortgage against the Rancho del Rosa, you said?"

Breen scowled thoughtfully. He had forgotten that mortgage. It must still be on the body of Sohmes. Not that it would do Breen any good to have it, but if it had never been recorded, he might be able to forge a transfer of it to himself from Sohmes. He decided to find out as soon as possible.

"There is a girl at the Rancho del Rosa," said Lee Duck.

Breen looked at the Chinaman, but did not reply.

"Her name is McKee," said the Chinaman.

"McKee? What McKee?"

"I have only the name. She is from Montana."

"The devil!" said Breen softly.

"Is she a daughter of Scotty McKee?"

"How do I know?" snarled Breen. "What if she is?"

"You are drinking too much," said the Chinaman. "It is not good for your nerves."

"Damn you, what are my nerves to you? I'll run my own affairs. I don't need any advice from a Chinaman."

Breen left the cantina and went down to Gomez's old adobe home, where he found Gomez and two of his men. Gomez's left eye was bandaged, as was his right cheek, and he could hardly see anything with his right eye.

"What brings you back here?" asked Gomez testily.

"I have decided," replied Breen, "that we must stand together, Lobo."

The Mexican grunted softly, wondering what had changed Breen's ideas.

"I told you I would pay one thousand pesos for the redhead."

"Yes."

"Could you raid the Rancho del Rosa quietly? Have you enough men to do the job? No killing, no burning, remember."

Gomez grinned. "I have a dozen men at my command."

"Not enough. Four cowboys could whip your dozen."

"Perhaps a surprise—"

"No perhaps."

"You have five good men."

"Certainly. I have five Americanos," meaningly.

"I could get more men—at a price."

"Get them. I will move my men to town and turn the rancho over to you and your men. Go slowly. Tell your men nothing, until the right time, and tell them that you will shoot the first man who disobeys the order not to shoot nor burn, unless something unforeseen happens."

"All this for one redhead?"

"You will get your orders, when you have all the men at my rancho."

"And the price you offer?"

"That can be settled at the same time. My men will come in from the rancho in the morning, and I will quarter them here in town; so that you and your men may move in at the rancho at once."

"At last you are showing some sense," growled Gomez. The idea of a raid appealed to him. He didn't like the idea of no shooting nor burning; but that could be handled. He had always been able to lie out of any situation; and he didn't like Breen very well, anyway.

Brick and Johnny went slowly along the old trail. They had no way of knowing how many more men might be at the Breen rancho, nor just where the place might be. Johnny watched the back trail pretty closely. He had no desire to be cut off from a chance to get back to that dry-wash, which was the nearest place they could head for the Border.

Finally they sighted the old huddle of adobe buildings, and worked their way to a closer view. Smoke was coming from a fireplace flue, but there was no sign of life. The six steers were still in the pole corral back of the houses.

"Let's go down and visit the place," suggested Brick.

"All right," dubiously. "There's somebody at home, that's a cinch."

They swung around the hill and came in from

the rear, passing the corral, where the six Diamond M steers were held. They dismounted quickly at an open door, and a frightened Chinaman met them, skillet in hand.

"Speak English?" snapped Brick.

"No sabe," quickly.

"Hablar Español?" asked Johnny.

"No entender."

"Prob'ly a damn liar on both counts," said Brick. "I suppose Breen and his men talk Chinese to the cook. Anybody home?" he asked the Chinaman, who began a sing-song explanation in Cantonese.

"Well, now that explains everythin'," grinned Brick, as he stepped in past the Chinaman, who moved back into the dirty kitchen.

"You watch our friend, while I search the place," said Brick.

But a search netted him nothing. The Chinaman was alone. He came back to the kitchen.

"You sabe Breen?" asked Brick.

The Chinaman looked blankly at him, nor did he change expression as Brick ran his hands over the folds of his shirt, looking for a knife or a gun. The Chinaman was unarmed.

"I reckon we'll collect our steers and head back," said Brick, and to the Chinaman, "When Breen comes, you tell him that the redhead took the beef back where it belongs, and that if Breen ever comes toward the Rancho del Rosa, the redhead will collect his ears."

Johnny translated it in halting Spanish, in case the Chinaman was able to understand that language; and then made the Chinaman go with them to the corral, where they released the steers.

"Never trust anybody down here," said Johnny wisely. "This blank-faced Celestial might shoot a thirty-thirty awful straight."

They said good-bye to the Chinaman and sent the steers galloping back down the trail, praying that they might reach the dry-wash without meeting anybody on the trail. And their prayers were granted. It was at least another hour before Lobo Gomez and eight of his men crossed the dry-wash, accompanied by Jim Breen.

Gomez's right eye was working pretty well, but the other was still bandaged heavily. Breen had decided to hurry the issue, and was going to the rancho with Gomez, where they were to decide on plans and payment. Breen had been drunk nearly all night, and was in a vile humor.

It was Gomez who first noted the absence of the six steers. Breen swore angrily, thinking that some of his own men might have turned them loose. They rode up to the house, and the Chinaman came out.

"Who turned them steers loose?" asked Breen, speaking in English.

The Chinaman shrugged his thin shoulders, as he replied:

"Man say, yo' tell Bleen ledhead take cow—"

"Wait a minute!" snorted Breen. "What man said this?"

"Ledhead plenty talk. He say yo' tell Bleen ledhead take cow back. He say yo' tell Bleen ledhead cut off ea's, if he come afte' cow."

"Speak Spanish!" roared Gomez. "Damn the English."

"That redhead has been here," said Breen harshly. "He took the steers back across the border, and left word that he'd cut off my ears if I came back after them."

Gomez laughed. He had no morals of any kind, but he couldn't help admiring this redhead, whom he had never seen.

"Said he would cut off my ears, eh?" gritted Breen. "We'll see about that pretty damn quick. Was he alone?"

"One mo' man. He call him Johnny."

"Johnny Snow. How long have they been gone?"

"Plenty long time."

Breen grunted sourly. Again the redhead had bested him. And worse than that, they had robbed the rancho of fresh meat. Gomez realized it too.

"It is bad," he admitted. "Maxwell has sent all his beef to the north ranges, where it would be difficult for us to take them away."

"He will pay," growled Breen. "And he will pay dearly."

"True," grinned Gomez. "They will surely pay well. The men will put up the horses, while we have plenty to drink and much to talk about."

And while Breen and Gomez laid their plans, Brick and Johnny took the six steers back to the Maxwell range, and went to the ranch, where Brick told Maxwell of their trip and its results.

"I want to thank you, Davidson," said Maxwell, "but never do anything as foolish as that again. No man's life is worth the price of a few steers; and you are taking your life in your hand when you go down there."

"It was worth the chance," grinned Brick. "I'd like to see their faces, when they discover the loss. I left word with the Chinese cook to tell Breen if he came up here, I'd remove his ears."

"I doubt if Breen had anything to do with the actual stealing of the steers."

"They were at what he calls his ranch. Mebby he wasn't one of the rustlers, but I'll bet he was goin' to eat the meat. And another thing, Mr. Maxwell," Brick lowered his voice. They were standing on the rear veranda, and a couple of the boys were watering horses at the well.

"We found the body of that man Sohmes to-day, away down there in a big dry-wash. He had been shot in the back of the head, and I'd say he had been murdered and robbed. I brought this much back, in case yuh want to give it to his relatives."

Brick took out the platinum watch and handed

it to the amazed ranch owner.

"Do you mean—they murdered Sohmes?" blankly.

Brick nodded slowly. "We buried him the best we could, but I found this in his hip-pocket."

Brick took out the mortgage and handed it to Maxwell, who stared at it blankly, hardly realizing what it was. Slowly he sat down on the top step, looking at the mortgage.

"I—I don't understand," he muttered. "You found this mortgage in his pocket?"

"And it ain't got a mark on it to show that Sohmes ever filed it."

"I can find out in San Francisco," said Maxwell slowly. "He wouldn't be foolish enough not to file it. And this watch? It has his initials on the back—H. S. You can't be mistaken, can you?"

"There was a couple of letters and a notebook. He was a fat man and wore glasses."

"Oh, it must be Sohmes."

"But about that mortgage," said Brick. "Wouldn't it have to be recorded in this county—at Sicomoro?"

"Why, certainly. I never thought of that."

"And they'd mark it with the number of the record book and all that. I tell yuh, that mortgage never was recorded."

"Do you suppose that could be possible?"

"We'll wait and see."

"But about the body; hadn't I better notify the

sheriff?"

"And do a lot of explainin'?"

"That is true," thoughtfully. "But to think of a man I knew, buried out there—"

"Let's forget it. You can't afford to explain. It might be better to hide that watch, and let the whole thing die down."

"Perhaps that is right."

"Nobody, except you and me and Johnny know about it. Johnny won't say a word, and it's a cinch the man who murdered him won't tell it."

For a long time Bob Maxwell stood there, the mortgage and the watch held tightly in his two hands. Then—

"Davidson, I guess you know how I feel. I want to play square. This mortgage was taken in good faith. It belongs to Sohmes."

"Sohmes was a crook. He paid you that money to use in a crooked game. He has prob'ly swindled the Government out of a lot of money. Mebby he didn't want that mortgage on record. He didn't want anybody to know about that money, and he figured this deal would put you on yore feet and pay off that mortgage right away. I'll betcha he never told anybody about the deal. Forget it. If nobody squawks about it, you keep the rancho and yore money."

Brick walked away, leaving Maxwell looking after him.

In the mean time Breen had concluded his

business with Lobo Gomez, and was on his way back to Gomez Springs alone. He wanted to make another search of Sohmes's body, in hopes of finding that mortgage. He knew a man who could do queer things with a pen, and for a few dollars this man could make an assignment of the mortgage in such a clever way that any one on earth, not an expert on handwriting, would accept it as the writing of Hubert Sohmes.

Breen had imbibed quite a lot of tequila before he left the rancho, but he was not drunk. He found the exact spot where he had left the body of Sohmes, but the body was not there. He found the notebook and the two letters, lodged against the mesquite brush, but the body was gone.

It rather upset Breen. He discovered quite a number of footprints in the sand, showing high heels. That made things look bad. Then he saw the mound of stones, where Brick and Johnny had buried Sohmes. But Breen was too tipsy and frightened to remove all those stones; so he managed to mount his horse and headed for Gomez Springs at a gallop.

Down in his heart he knew that the redhead had found the body. They had taken the stolen cattle down that wash and had made the discovery.

"If Gomez don't make good, I'll kill him myself," he swore. "I've got to get rid of him. I'll nail his scalp to the front door of the rancho, the meddling fool."

CHAPTER XII

SILENT WARNS THE RANCHO DEL ROSA

BRICK had been doing a lot of thinking over things which had happened since he came to the Rancho del Rosa, and the next day he said to Johnny Snow, as they worked around the stable:

"What ever became of Dell Harper's horse and saddle after he was killed?"

"Oh, we found the horse. The saddle was gone, and we decided that the animal had rolled it off. We never did find the saddle. I remember it very well—an old black hull, Visalia tree, made in Oregon, I think. Yeah, it was a G. L. saddle, made in Portland."

Brick examined his own saddle, but found no trade-mark on it.

"I'll betcha that saddle was made in Gomez Springs," said Johnny. "Old man Beeman was the saddle-maker in Sicomoro, but he got into some kinda trouble a year or so ago and moved down there. It shore looks like some of his work. He makes good saddles. It was originally decorated, yuh can see where the ornaments was fastened on. Beeman was pretty good on silver trimmin'."

"Can he make a livin' down there?" asked Brick.

"Well, he can keep out of jail," grinned Johnny.

That afternoon Brick rode to Sicomoro and sauntered around to the sheriff's little adobe office, where he found the sheriff alone, enjoying an old cob pipe. The little old office was almost entirely papered with old reward notices, many of them bearing the pictured likeness of the man wanted.

"I've been wonderin' why yuh didn't come up and see me," said Campbell. "I see Joe Pico is walkin' around again, but he's pretty tame."

"I hope he's tame," grinned Brick. "I don't want any more trouble with him. How is everythin' goin' in yore business?"

"It's about the same old thing every day."

"You shore do get plenty reward notices, judgin' from yore walls."

The sheriff laughed as he refilled his pipe.

"That's Ortego's idea—paperin' the walls. Yeah, wc do get plenty. Yuh see, this is sort of a clearin'-house for criminals. Lots of 'em head for the Border, and they don't dare go through a regular port of entry; so they hunt for the wide Border. It's shore plenty wide down here. And when a new notice shows up, Ortego pastes it over an old one. Kinda keeps yuh up to date, yuh see."

Brick started to grin, but his blue eyes grew serious, as his gaze shifted to a notice about midway up a wall. It was from Sun Dog County, offering five thousand dollars reward for Arthur B. Slade, dead or alive.

There was no picture, but the description was accurate. Convicted of murder in the first degree, it said.

Brick shifted his eyes away from it and began rolling a cigarette.

"The first day I saw you, yuh asked me about Jim Breen," said the sheriff. "Didja ever meet him?"

"Yeah, I saw him," nodded Brick. "Quite a character. He'd be a good man for you to stand in with, it seems to me. Down there in his town, he ought to be able to keep cases on a lot of men."

The sheriff squinted one eye and looked sideways at Brick.

"He didn't tell you that, did he?"

"No-o-o; I was just thinkin' he could."

"He could—but he hasn't. He used to come in here and look over the reward notices once in a while."

The sheriff laughed softly, as he lighted a match with a snap of his thumb-nail.

"He shore overlooked one bet a few days ago and lost a nice piece of change for himself. See that notice up there—about the middle of the wall, the one from up in Montana? The man rode in here with Breen one day. I'd bet ten dollars against one that he's the man. Ortego had pasted the notice, before I had ever seen it.

"This feller was so darned big that I got to

thinkin' him over, after he was gone, and about that time I saw this new notice. Breen jist lost five thousand. Dead or alive, that's how bad they want *him*."

"And Breen didn't bring him back again, eh?"

"I haven't even seen Breen since that day."

"And you can't go to Mexico and get a man."

"Well," smiled the sheriff, "I never have. It seems to me that there's a law against such a thing. How's everythin' at Maxwell's place?"

"All right."

"Somebody was tellin' me that a Miss McKee is out there. I wonder if she's any relation to Scotty McKee, who used to live here?"

"She's a nice-lookin' girl."

The sheriff got up from his chair, plucked a straw from a broom in the corner, and began cleaning the stem of his pipe. When he sat down again and relighted his pipe, Brick drew a chair in close to the desk.

"You've known Breen a long time, Sheriff?" he asked.

"Quite a few years—yes."

"Why did Scotty McKee leave here suddenly?"

The sheriff looked curiously at Brick, wondering what this red-headed cowboy was driving at.

"I dunno," he replied.

"Yuh do know that he left here suddenly, don'tcha?"

"I know he did. In fact, he never told anybody good-bye."

"Have you ever known Breen to take a trip North? Mebby gone for a couple of weeks, or longer?"

"No, I don't know anythin' about that. Sometimes there's a month or more that I don't even see him. He's runnin' a business down in Gomez Springs, yuh know."

"Yeah, I know that. Was him and Scotty McKee good friends?"

"I can't answer that; they knew each other. But what is the idea of all these questions, Davidson?"

Brick rolled another cigarette, his jaw tensed just a little, as he debated things over. Campbell struck him as being a square-shooter, an efficient officer in a land where men must be efficient.

"That notice yuh spoke about up there," said Brick softly, "is for the man who was convicted of the murder of Scotty McKee."

"The murder of Scotty McKee? Why, I never heard—wait a minute."

The sheriff closed the door and came back to his desk.

"I want to get this straight," he said. "Yuh see, I liked Scotty."

"I liked him, too," said Brick slowly. "Yuh see, I was the sheriff of Sun Dog, where Scotty was murdered. They convicted Slade of the murder, and I turned him loose."

"Well, my God!" The sheriff gawped at Brick. "Wasn't that a funny thing for a sheriff to do?"

"I was a funny sheriff, I reckon."

And then Brick started at the beginning and told the sheriff what happened, from the time Scotty McKee bought the ranch in Sun Dog until he (Brick) resigned his office and came South. It took at least a half hour for Brick to finish his tale. The sheriff filled his pipe and smoked for a while.

"I dunno," he said, after a long silence. "I kinda figure that yore conscience is the best judge. If yore conscience says you've done the right thing, it's right. You didn't believe Slade killed McKee. I can see yore argument. I'm gettin' to the age where I can set down and look at the other feller's angle on things. To the satisfaction of the law, they say. To satisfy a few printed words.

"Davidson, I believe in right and wrong. Don't mistake me in that. But the law can be just as wrong as an individual. Judges and juries can be wrong, and when twelve men are wrong, it's jist too bad. This man Slade was yore best friend, you say. If he had been yore enemy, would you have believed him innocent? Look at that angle."

"Where did the letters addressed to Jim Breen, and the sack of marahuana come from?"

193

"Do you think Breen is a murderer?" countered the sheriff.

"I know damn well he is! No, I can't tell yuh how I know. You've got to prove a thing like that—and I can't prove it."

"You know he killed Scotty McKee?"

"No, I don't *know* that."

The sheriff lighted his pipe again. This red-headed cowboy had him puzzled. Who did he think Breen had murdered, he wondered?

"Do you think Breen murdered Dell Harper, the man you found?"

"I don't believe he did, unless—"

"Unless what?"

"He came to the Rancho del Rosa after I got there that day, and Slade was with him. I don't believe Slade would have been a party to any murder. Of course, Breen might have been alone earlier in the day."

"Well, who do you think he murdered?"

"I can't tell you right now, Campbell."

The sheriff grunted softly and looked up at the reward notice. Then—

"Any time yuh need my help, don't forget to ask for it," he said. "You know Berry and Mitchell, the Border Patrol; they'll help yuh. I've got nothin' on Breen. He can go back and forth across the Border—but I'll keep an eye on him.

"He used to come down here quite often and talk with me. Seemed to be interested in reward notices. I suppose he kept sort of a check on those who came down in his country, and once in a while he'd tell me about some of 'em. It was handy information for me."

"Handy for him, too, I reckon," smiled Brick.

"In what way?"

"Wanted murderers are seldom spies of the Government."

"Oh!"

The sheriff didn't question Brick any further. He had long had a suspicion that Breen was mixed up in smuggling deals, but it was nothing more than a suspicion. Brick went from the sheriff's office to the One Oak Cantina. He had not been there since the day he won the horse and saddle from Joe Pico, and he wondered what kind of a reception he would get.

There were several men in the place, and among them was Edward Pico. He gave Brick a cordial "Bucnas dias," and invited him to have a drink. It rather surprised Brick, but he accepted.

"Never refuse the goodwill of the devil," he told himself.

"My brother is around again," he told Brick, as they filled their glasses, "but he bears no grudge."

"Well, that's fine," smiled Brick. "Sorry it happened. I'd rather be his friend than his enemy."

"Buena!"—only he pronounced it "Way-no,"

giving the soft Mexican slur to the word. "It was merely unfortunate. Joe is high-strung. And the two Abelardo brothers—they will annoy you no more. It was without my consent or knowledge that they went to the Rancho del Rosa that night."

Brick smiled over his drink, but said nothing. He didn't know whether Ed Pico was sincere, or whether he wanted to be sure that Brick had a hand in swinging Al and Bill from the oak limb that night.

"Everythin' is all right," he said, "and here's hopin' that it keeps on bein' right."

"That is very certain, my friend. I admire Roberto Maxwell, who is my old friend, although we have seen little of each other lately."

Brick was fairly sure that Ed Pico was the leader of the hijackers, and he wondered if Pico had any suspicions that Maxwell had ever been mixed up in a smuggling proposition. He decided that Pico was far from being a fool, and that no doubt he had spies in Gomez Springs. It was a game that required inside information ahead of time. He wondered how many spies Breen had in Sicomoro. Some, no doubt.

"You bought this cantina from Scotty McKee, didn't yuh?" asked Brick.

"Yes. Did you know him?"

"I knew him up in Montana."

"Yes? Montana, eh? He went a long ways from here."

"Was he in trouble when he left here?"

Pico looked sharply at Brick, who was looking directly at him. The Mexican shrugged his shoulders, smiling thinly.

"Who knows? A man's business is his own in this country. We do not ask a man if he is in trouble—that is his own affair."

"I reckon I asked a foolish question."

"One that only McKee could answer truthfully."

"Then it won't never be answered—McKee was murdered up in Montana several months ago."

"No!" Pico's surprise was genuine. "Murdered? By whom?"

Brick shook his head and motioned for the bartender to set out the bottle again.

"That is bad news," sighed Pico. "I liked Scotty McKee, although we were—" Pico stopped to fill his glass.

"You were not friends?" queried Brick.

"Friends—yes. Perhaps we differed in our views. And now he is dead. That is bad." He lifted his glass, "Mil afectos de mi parte. You do not understand Spanish? Pardon me. My kindest regards."

They drank together and Brick left the cantina. He met Joe Pico on the sidewalk. Joe looked thin and wan, but his eyes were bright.

"Buenas dias, pelo-rojo," he said. "Good-day, red-hair."

Brick grinned. Johnny Snow had called him "pelo-rojo."

"Glad to see yuh out again," nodded Brick. "Feelin' good?"

Joe nodded and went on into the cantina. But Brick wasn't deceived in the least by the pleasant manner of the Pico brothers. Brick knew that he was far from forgiven for shooting Joe, and that Joe would return the compliment at the best opportunity.

Wong Hop, fat and bland, stood in the doorway of his little adobe restaurant and watched Brick ride out of town. Many a smuggled Celestial had passed through Wong Hop's hands; but business had been bad of late. Wong Kee, his cousin, was dead, Lee Duck allied with Breen. It was not strange that Wong Hop had jumped to the other side of the fence and was furnishing Ed Pico with information. A man must live.

Lee Duck was rather disgusted with Jim Breen. Lee had lost a lot of money in the diamond fiasco, and he was not at all satisfied. Perhaps he talked too much to Louie Yen, a Chinese herb doctor, who was a good friend to Wong Hop. At any rate, Wong Hop had certain information, which might contain a grain of truth, and he explained it all to Ed Pico, who came to eat fried rice every day.

"You say they think Breen got the diamonds

himself, Wong?" queried Pico, speaking Spanish, which Wong spoke like a native.

"It sounds reasonable. Who else? And that something happened to Sohmes, the man from the North, who disposes of the diamonds. Sohmes came here, hired a horse and buggy and went to Gomez Springs. He sent the driver back with the vehicle, deciding to ride with Breen to his rancho. Lee Duck saw them go. Breen says that Sohmes did not go to the rancho, but that he came back here.

"No one saw him come back, and there is only one road. Lee Duck says Sohmes did not know the diamonds were missing. If he came down here to secure the diamonds, he carried thousands of dollars with him. The man was fat, unused to a saddle, and it does not stand to reason that he would go North on a horse, sneaking past Sicomoro, because he had nothing to conceal. Lee Duck thinks Breen had the diamonds all the time; that Breen conspired to get Wong Kee murdered, so that no man would know how the diamonds were sent. I do not know the truth, but that is as Louie Yen told it to me."

"And that Breen killed Sohmes for his money?"

"Perhaps. And also Breen is offering Gomez a reward for the redhead who works at the Rancho del Rosa."

Pico grinned widely. "What has he done to Breen?"

"Who knows? Perhaps it is because of Maxwell's daughter. It was said that she would wed Breen very soon; but Breen has been keeping away from the Rancho del Rosa since the redhead came."

"I haven't the heart to interfere," grinned Pico. "But I would like to get my hands on Breen. Where would he keep the diamonds?"

"He spends much time at his rancho, they say. You have been there?"

"I know it well. Perhaps—"

"He keeps five men at the rancho, but it is evident they have little stomach for fighting his battles. Just now they are all living in town."

"Why?"

"Perhaps Breen is keeping them amused, while he and that braggart of a Gomez stay at the rancho and plan their devilment. Breen is drinking heavily, and Gomez will keep pace with him."

Pico thanked Wong for the information and went back to talk it over with Joe.

Brick wondered if he had done right in making a confidant of the sheriff. Campbell seemed very human, but it was really the "dead or alive" notice that caused Brick to tell the story. He felt that if the sheriff understood Brick's angle on the matter, he might give Silent more consideration, in case the big cowboy came across the border.

Juanita told Brick that day she would be going back to Montana in a few days. She had tried to induce Marie to go back with her, but with little success. Brick tried to plan out some way in which Silent might get a few words with Juanita, but there did not seem to be any way. Silent could not take a chance on crossing the line, and Mexico, just at the point, was no place for Juanita.

"You'll come back to Sun Dog some day," Juanita told him.

"I don't think so. There's nothin' in Sun Dog for me. I couldn't even get a job at forty a month in Sun Dog."

"Soapy Caswell would hire you, Brick."

"Out of pity—he might. Good old Soapy. No, I'll stay down here. There's a lot of cow country down along this border. Are you goin' to run the ranch, when you go back?"

"Why not?"

"Oh, you'll prob'ly marry some Sun Dog cattleman."

"Brick!"

"I'm sorry."

"Silent will come back some day."

"I wish I had yore confidence."

The big yellow moon was shining over the patio wall, flooding the flagged paths with light.

Over in the bunk-house, Johnny Snow was strumming "La Paloma," while a mocking-bird in the roses called, *Peter, Peter, Peter, Peter,* in a sleepy voice. Old Mujer in the kitchen was singing softly, as she finished her work.

"I think I am afraid of this country," said Juanita.

"Afraid of what?"

"Oh, I don't know; but I have always the feeling that something will happen. Nothing has, of course. I suppose I am foolish. Marie laughs at me; laughs at the idea of anything out of the ordinary happening at the Rancho del Rosa. But it is lonesome, Brick. No neighbors, no other women."

"Yeah, that's true. I've noticed—" Brick stopped short. A man had stepped in through the rose-covered archway and had stopped just inside the patio. His shadow looked big and grotesque against the old patio wall.

Brick got slowly to his feet, scraping his boot against the worn tile of the steps. The man swung around and came toward them. They were standing in the full light of the moon, and he stopped a few steps away, staring at them.

"Juanita?" he said hoarsely. "You—it can't be you?"

It was Silent Slade.

"Hello, pardner," said Brick softly, but Silent ignored him. Juanita was leaning forward, her eyes wide in the moonlight.

"Silent," she said, whispering his name. "Where in the world?"

And then he took her in his arms, mumbling to himself. He had been clean-shaved, and looked like the old Silent Slade, as he held out his hand to Brick.

"I had to come," he said simply. "They're framin' to get you, pardner, and I had to pack a warnin'."

"Who?" asked Brick.

"Breen and Gomez. I'm part of Breen's gang. You've got him scared, and he's goin' to try and bush yuh."

"When?"

"Quien sabe?"

Silent laughed softly and turned to Juanita, who was looking at him dumbly, hardly realizing that it really was Silent Slade.

"Yuh see, I'm learnin' Español, Honey," he said.

"Oh, Silent, I can hardly believe my eyes. It really is you?"

"And all in one chunk. Good Lord, I'd have been here long ago, if I had known you was here. Tell me about it. Brick, can't we go somewhere and talk? You know there's a reward—"

"Forget it," growled Brick. "Maxwell is a friend. The boys here are all square-shooters. The sheriff—"

"Knows I'm down in Gomez Springs," laughed Silent. "Breen told me."

"Breen prob'ly told him, too."

"Shore. Breen is as crooked as a pretzel. Oh, don't I know that hombre? Me and him almost had a run-in the other night. He's pretty close-mouthed, but I found out that him and Gomez want to get yuh. His men are all in Gomez Springs, drunk most of the time."

"Do any of 'em know you came?"

"Kelsey does. He was almost sober. I reckon Breen gave him orders to see that none of us got our horses from the stable, but I got mine. I told Kelsey I was comin' across the line. He asked me the other day if I knew you. I reckon it was because I told Breen to lay off you, or get his hands crooked to handle a harp."

The bunk-house door slammed and Johnny Snow came across the patio, humming a tune. He came up to the group and Brick introduced him to Silent. In a few words he told Johnny who Silent was and why he was there.

"That's great," said Johnny. "But the warnin' is old stuff, Slade. Me and Brick knowed that Breen was after us. Yuh see, we took back them six beeves that Gomez and his gang ran across the Border."

Silent hadn't heard about that, because he and the other boys left that same morning, and it made him laugh.

"I'd like to have heard Breen, when he found it out. And that danged Chink can talk both

English and Spanish. He shore could deliver yore message."

"We was sure of that. Where's yore horse?"

"Just outside the patio."

"I'll bring him in, Slade. Yuh never know when yuh might need a horse real quick."

"He's one of our own kind," said Brick, as Johnny went after the horse. "The kid has shore got the stuff."

Marie heard them talking and came out on the porch. She was almost as surprised as Juanita, when Juanita introduced her to Silent. They were all trying to talk at once, when Johnny came back with the horse. He dropped the reins near the steps and walked around on the moonlit side of the animal, examining the saddle. Finally he came back to them.

"Slade," he said softly, "where didja get that saddle?"

"I suppose it belongs to Breen."

"What about it?" asked Brick quickly.

"That was Dell Harper's saddle. I'd know it anywhere."

Brick walked out and looked it over. It was as Johnny had described it to him; an old black leather saddle, Visalia tree, made by the G. L. Company, Portland, Oregon.

"Can yuh find out where Breen got it?" asked Johnny.

"Well, I shore can try it," replied Silent. "Some

205

of the boys might know about it. Breen furnishes horses and ridin' rigs."

"How long can you stay?" asked Juanita, who was more interested in that than in the saddle.

"You shore don't have to run," said Johnny. "Won't nobody know yo're here, Slade."

Marie took Brick by the arm and squeezed softly, as she whispered:

"Bring Johnny in the house. Can't you see they want to be alone?"

"Look out!" hissed Johnny.

A man was riding through the archway. Johnny stepped in against Silent, shoving him back into the deep foliage, which screened the porch.

"Get down!" he hissed, and then aloud, "Well, I better put that horse away," and walked out to the animal.

The rider dismounted near the steps. It was Campbell, the sheriff. He paid no attention to Johnny and the horse, but came up to the three people on the steps.

"Hello, folks," he said pleasantly.

The girls were tongue-tied.

"Oh, hello, Sheriff," said Brick. "Had yore back to the moon, and I didn't recognize yuh. How are yuh?"

"Finer 'n frawg-hair."

He stopped on the lower step and wiped his face with a handkerchief.

"Just ridin' around, and stopped to say howdy. Is Maxwell at home?"

"Ye—yes, he is in the house," stammered Marie. "I'll go in with you."

"Thank yuh kindly. Kinda warm this evenin', ain't it?"

"Sultry," said Brick. "Might storm."

"Shore might. I'll see yuh later."

Marie took him into the house and closed the door. Silent got to his feet, took a deep breath, and holstered his gun. He had been all ready.

"Me for room enough to turn around in," he said softly. "Every rose has its thorns, and these back in that bush has a-plenty."

"You and Juanita go out the back gate," said Brick. "That'll give yuh a getaway. When yuh hear me whistle, like I was callin' a dog—you hit the grit."

Silent took his horse, and went cautiously across the patio with Juanita, while Brick and Johnny sat down on the steps.

"Gosh, what a close call!" said Johnny. "It's a darned good thing Campbell wasn't lookin' for Slade."

"I'd tell a man," grinned Brick. "Good for both of 'em. I don't think Silent Slade would ever give up without a scrap."

"What do yuh reckon he wants to see Maxwell for? It ain't often that he comes here."

"I dunno."

They sat there in the moonlight, smoking and listening to the night-birds. Just inside the main room they could hear the sheriff talking with Marie and her father, and a few minutes later Marie came out with the sheriff.

Brick heard them coming, and he whistled sharply several times, as though calling a dog. They came to the steps and the sheriff put on his big hat.

"Could I speak privately to yuh for a minute, Davidson?" he asked.

"Why, shore," replied Brick, wondering what the sheriff had on his mind. They walked out to the sheriff's horse, and the sheriff lowered his voice, as he said:

"Breen came to Sicomoro to-night. He told me that I'd find Slade here."

"Yea-a-ah?"

"I didn't find him here. Breen must have been mistaken."

"Must have been," said Brick slowly.

"I dunno why Breen told me this."

"I dunno, Sheriff."

"I reckon Slade has been workin' for Breen."

"That might be true."

"Uh-huh. And Slade ought to know that Breen tried to turn him in, but I don't reckon there'll be any chance to tell him —not since you whistled to the dog. Yuh see, I happen to know that there never has been a dog on this rancho."

The sheriff slowly mounted his horse and adjusted his hat.

"Do yuh know if Breen is still in Sicomoro?" asked Brick.

"He was there when I left; he may wait to see me come back."

"Thank yuh kindly, Sheriff."

"Yo're welcome. Good-night, folks," he called to Brick and Marie, and rode out of the patio.

Juanita had evidently been watching from the rear gate, and after the sheriff rode away, she came back across the patio.

"Has he gone?" asked Brick.

"Yes," she said softly. "He heard your signal. Oh, I'm so glad I saw him. He says he will come back again. Did the sheriff suspect anything?"

"Not a thing."

Brick turned and started for the stable alone, but Johnny joined him near the gate.

"What's up?" asked Johnny.

"Breen is in Sicomoro. He came there to warn the sheriff that Silent came here to-night; and I'm goin' to have a showdown with Mr. Breen."

"Are yuh goin' to Sicomoro, Brick?"

"Right now."

"I'll go with yuh—he might have a friend with him."

CHAPTER XIII

THE PICOS PLAY A HUNCH

SILENT had misjudged Kelsey. The skinny outlaw met Breen shortly after Silent's departure for the Rancho del Rosa, and they had a few more drinks which caused Kelsey to talk confidentially to Breen. Perhaps Kelsey figured he owed more to Breen than he did to Slade, and Kelsey was the type that makes good stool-pigeons. So he told Breen that Slade had taken a horse and gone to Maxwell's place.

For several minutes Breen was profanely bitter. He cursed Kelsey for letting Slade have a horse and saddle, but Kelsey pointed out that Slade was nearly twice his size, and that it might be better for all concerned, if Slade didn't know that Breen had heard of his absence.

Then Breen got a bright idea. He would go to Sicomoro, tell the sheriff where he could catch Slade, and thereby remove Slade from their midst. So he saddled a horse and nearly ran its legs off in getting to Sicomoro, where he told the sheriff, who lost no time in heading for the rancho.

Breen wanted to be sure that the sheriff captured Slade, before he went back to Gomez Springs; so he sauntered around Sicomoro, killing time. He had a few drinks in a little cantina at the end of the main street, where he saw Al Abelardo. Breen had always detested the half-breed, who left the cantina on Breen's arrival.

He came on up to another cantina, and met Joe Pico on the adobe walk in front of the place. Breen spoke to Joe, who merely nodded. Breen had a drink, lighted one of his own brand of cigarettes, and went out, heading for the One Oak Cantina, further up the street.

But Jim Breen didn't get that far. As he passed a narrow alley, he met a man in the dark; a man who was evidently intoxicated. The walk was narrow, and they almost collided. Breen stopped short, and as he stopped, something crashed down on his head from behind, and Breen lost all interest in things.

That is, he lost interest for ten or fifteen minutes, in which time his locale was considerably changed. He awoke with a dull ache in his head and a feeling that he had been eating salt. He was lying on an old couch, near a table, on which rested an oil-lamp with a smoky chimney. Seated beside him was Bill Abelardo, gun in hand, while Al Abelardo was seated across the table, his elbows resting on the table, a grin on his thin features. Breen grunted and tried to sit up, but found that he was roped to the old couch.

"Fill pretty good, eh?" grinned Al.

"What's the idea?" gritted Breen. He had little love for these two men—and they knew it.

"Theese idea ees good one," grinned Al.

"Damn half-breed!" groaned Breen. "Which one of you hit me? I'll pay you back for this."

The Abelardos laughed joyfully.

"He's make pay for theese, eh?" grinned Al. "Mucho buena."

"Damn good!" chuckled Bill.

Breen heard a footstep, and turned his head to see Ed Pico coming across the room. He halted at the end of the couch and looked at Breen.

"This is some of your work, eh?" gritted Breen.

Pico inhaled deeply on a cigarette, nodding slowly, his dark eyes flashing in the yellow light.

"What's the big idea?" asked Breen.

"The big idea," said Pico slowly, "is that you are tied up. I have plenty evidence that you murdered a man named Sohmes. Makes you flinch, eh? Why not? The sheriff would be glad to know what I have heard. Sohmes was a citizen of this country—and you are on the north side of the line."

Breen wet his dry lips with a dryer tongue, as he wondered what this man *knew*. He had no wish to try and prove his innocence.

"What's your game, Pico?" he asked hoarsely. "This idea of knocking me on the head, roping me from head to heel, and then accusing me of a

212

murder I know nothing about. As far as I know, Sohmes is alive."

Pico laughed. He knew better. Breen's eyes shifted nervously.

"The murder is already proved," he lied coldly. "The question is this, How much is it worth to you to save your own neck?"

"Staging a hold-up, eh?"

"Call it what you will."

"Damn you, what do you want? How much? I'm not a rich man, but—"

"But you do not want to talk with the sheriff. Is that it? They hang men for murder down here."

Breen gritted his teeth and stared at the ceiling, wondering what it was all about. He turned his eyes and looked at Pico.

"Well, go ahead and talk. You've hijacked plenty of stuff from me. We know each other. What's the price, Pico?"

"Those diamonds."

"Diamonds, eh?"

"The ones Dell Harper was supposed to bring across. Either you or one of your men killed him, I suppose. But he didn't have them, Breen. You got them from Wong Kee, and then had Wong Kee murdered. We want those diamonds, or you get a bed in jail to-night, charged with the murder of Sohmes."

Breen blinked thoughtfully. He had the keen

mind of a fox, and now he could see a way out. He would outwit these slow thinkers.

"You have searched me?" he asked.

Pico nodded coldly. "We didn't expect you to carry them, Breen."

Breen laughed softly in spite of his aching head.

"No doubt you will let me go and get them for you."

"Exactly—but not alone. They are in Gomez Springs?"

"No."

"At your rancho?"

Breen shut his lips tightly, refusing to answer.

"How many men have you at the rancho?"

"My men are all in Gomez Springs," sullenly. "But that does you no good. None of them know where the stuff is hidden, and I'll see you damned, before I tell. You haven't any evidence against me, Pico. Your bluff is no good."

Ed Pico smiled, as he rolled a fresh cigarette.

"You call it bluff, eh?" he mused. "Perhaps it is. All I have is the word of other men. They are willing to testify. It seems that they have no friendship for you, and would like to see you hung. I do not consider your life worth one tenth of the diamonds—but you possibly have a different idea of its value. The owner of a life usually does value it more than any one else would. But that is final, Breen. You take us to the

214

diamonds, hand them over to us, and you go free. A crooked move, and we kill you on the spot. Consider all this, and give me your answer."

"Suppose I split the diamonds with you, Pico?"

"Would you split, if you were in my place? Yes? You liar! You'd take them all, and slit my throat in the bargain. Perhaps you'll save your throat; it all depends. You see, I have never murdered a man—yet."

Breen shut his eyes and for several minutes there was no word spoken. His head seemed filled with trip-hammers, but it did not affect the functioning of his crooked brain. Finally he opened his eyes.

"It's nothing but a damn hold-up," he said wearily. "But what can I do? Take these ropes off and I'll take you to the diamonds."

Pico laughed at Breen. "Take off what ropes? You fool, did you think we would turn you loose? You'll take us to the diamonds all right, but you'll be roped all the time. I'd trust you about as far as I'd trust a snake."

Al and Bill unroped him from the couch, but immediately bound his arms tightly to his body and took a half-hitch around his neck. They found Joe Pico outside with the five horses, and they immediately tied Breen to the saddle. Al Abelardo tied the lead rope to his saddle-horn, and they headed for the Border. They had held Breen in the Pico home in Sicomoro.

Breen was no fool, and he thought he had fooled Ed Pico. He knew that Lobo Gomez would have a guard out at the rancho, who would hear them coming. Unless the newcomers announced who they were, Gomez was to take it for granted that they were enemies, and act accordingly. Breen's only chance for failure would be that Gomez might show a light at the rancho, and cause his captors to show undue caution, or that the guard might have imbibed too much tequila. Ed Pico led the way. He knew where to hit the old dry-wash and cut the trail to the rancho, because he had been there many times. All four men were armed with rifles, in addition to their revolvers, but Breen was not afraid. Lobo Gomez had just cause to hate the Pico and Abelardo family, and Breen wondered just what the big bandit would do to them. It would be plenty, he decided.

Brick and Johnny arrived at Sicomoro just after the sheriff got there, but they didn't find Jim Breen. They searched all the cantinas and went through all the stores, but they didn't catch sight of the dapper personage they sought.

Later they came back to the sheriff's office and sat with him for a while. He hadn't seen Breen, and he confessed that it seemed queer. He was sure that Breen would wait and see if Slade was captured. He didn't ask them why they followed him to Sicomoro, because he knew they wouldn't tell him, and because it was none of his business.

They drifted back along the street, keeping their eyes open, listening to the conversation in the stores and cantinas, which netted them nothing.

"It's kinda funny we ain't seen none of the Pico outfit," declared Johnny. "Yuh usually see some of them around here."

"The less I see of that outfit, the better I like it, Johnny."

"Me, too; only I thought it was kinda queer."

Johnny casually inquired of the bartender in the One Oak if Pico was around, but the bartender didn't know.

"He was here a while ago," he said. "Come in pretty soon, I guess."

But Pico didn't come. They played roulette for a while, but their luck was bad, and they made another circle of the town, finally coming back to their horses.

"Well, that son of a gun got away," said Brick wearily. "I shore did hanker to meet him. I was goin' to knock his nose so far around on his face that he'd have to lay down on his back to smell of a rose."

"He's shore got somethin' comin'," laughed Johnny. "I shore hope I'm in sight when it happens."

They mounted and rode back to the rancho. Some thunderheads had come up from the west and obscured the moon. Heat lightning played along the distant hills, and the air was oppressive.

"We're due for a storm," said Johnny. "Don't get much rain this time of the year, but all this heat is shore to stir up a thunder storm."

They rode slowly along the dusty road. It was too sultry to think of sleeping; so they were in no hurry. It was quite dark when they reached the rancho and stabled their horses. Brick lighted a lantern in the stable, noting that it was nearly twelve o'clock by his watch.

"Everybody's gone to bed, I guess," said Johnny. "Slim will jist about wake up and howl like a wolf. I never did see a man who hated to wake up as bad as Slim."

"Maybe we better take the lantern," grinned Brick. "Save us from fallin' over a chair when we try to find the lamp."

"Good idea. C'mon."

They went through the rear arch and into the patio, the lantern throwing long shadows from their moving legs, as they headed for the bunkhouse door. Suddenly Brick jerked to a stop, Johnny bumped into him and dropped the lantern, which was immediately extinguished, leaving them in darkness.

It came again, that queer noise, which Brick had heard.

"F'r God's sake!" grunted Johnny. "What'sat, Brick?"

It was more or less of a hollow groan, just ahead of them in the darkness. Brick ripped a match along the leg of his overalls, cupping the light in his palms.

"Get the lantern, Johnny!" he blurted. "It's Slim! Hold it still, can'tcha? My gosh, I can't light it on the fly, can I?"

Brick managed to light the wick and squeak the chimney back into place. It was Slim Neeley, his face clotted with blood, hair matted, on his hands and knees. Brick handed the lantern to Johnny, picked Slim up under the arms and kicked the bunk-house door open ahead of him. He put Slim on a bunk, where the foreman of the Rancho del Rosa proceeded to sag back in a faint.

Brick lighted the lamp, grabbed the lantern and went running to the house, with Johnny at his heels. The back door was wide open, and they went in on the run. Old Mujer, the Mexican-Indian cook, was roped to a chair, tightly gagged with an old apron.

Brick quickly took away the gag and the ropes, questioning her, shaking her by the shoulder, but she merely looked blankly at them, working her mouth foolishly.

"Gag was too tight; she can't speak!" panted Johnny, as he lighted a lamp on the table.

Brick was halfway up the stairs before Johnny got the lamp lighted. Everything was confusion up there. The rooms had been turned upside down, and everything was strewn around, furniture smashed. Brick ran down to Johnny, his face white in the yellow light.

"Nobody up there?" whispered Johnny. Brick shook his head, as he braced one hand against the table, looking at the old woman.

"She can't talk," said Johnny. "Never could talk much. Let's see if Slim knows anythin'."

They went back to the bunk-house, where Brick poured water on Slim's head and wiped him off with a towel. The water brought Slim back to consciousness. He had been hit over the head pretty hard. Brick gave him a drink of water and his eyes gradually assumed a normal expression.

"Remember what happened, Slim?" asked Brick.

Slim blinked thoughtfully and his hand reached up to feel of his head. He seemed to have difficulty in figuring out what was the matter. He frowned up at the two boys, sighed deeply, and looked at his hands.

"Don'tcha remember anythin', Slim?" pleaded Johnny.

"Have I been sick?" he asked weakly. "I—I don't remember—"

"Yuh got hurt. Don'tcha remember gettin' hurt, Slim? Somebody must have hit yuh over the head. Did somebody come here—?"

Slim was staring at him, wide-eyed. He remembered now.

"Mexicans," he said slowly. "The place was full of 'em. My God, what happened? I was in the house, and—and when I came out—they met me at the door. They had rifles. I—I remember now, tryin' to pull a gun. But I don't remember whether I pulled it or not."

"Somebody popped yuh on the head."

"That's funny. But what happened? Give me another drink, will yuh? I'm so danged thirsty, and my head hurts. What happened?"

Brick gave him a drink and he gulped thirstily.

"That's good water," said Slim wearily. "It hits the spot."

"Yo're lucky to have any spot to hit. And all you know is that you saw a lot of Mexicans, eh?"

"It's jist like a dream. Lot of Mexicans with rifles. Shore surprised me, I tell yuh. I wasn't dreamin' it was I?"

"I reckon you wasn't," said Johnny. "There's nobody left, except you and Mujer. They gagged her so tight that she can't talk."

"Everybody gone?" Slim sat up dizzily. Brick and Johnny nodded.

"A—a raid, eh? Oh, that's a hell of a note! And me knocked down—"

"They probably thought yuh was dead," said Brick. "You better lay down and take care of that head."

"Everythin' goes around and around—" and Slim went out again.

Brick and Johnny looked at each other. Never in Brick's life had he felt as helpless as he did this moment. Marie, Juanita, Maxwell, Buck Eads, and Leo Herrera—all missing. Where and why?

The sound of a step at the doorway, and they whirled. It was only old Mujer, her dirty face streaked with tears. She came in, walking painfully.

"Can yuh talk now, Mujer?" asked Johnny.

"Talk little," she said thickly.

"What happened? You saw it all?"

"Not see much. Two Mejicanos come in kitchen, tie me up. Tie apron in mouth, some over face. Can't see. Hear much noise. Take me in room and tie me on chair. Hear plenty, see nothing. Marie cry."

The old woman put her hands over her face.

"Keep talkin'," said Johnny huskily. "What else didja hear?"

"Too much talk. They all go way, leave me on chair."

"Do yuh know who it was, Mujer?" asked Brick.

"Don't know. Not see. Too many talk." She took away her hands and looked at Slim.

"He dead?"

"No, he's all right; just hit on the head. Pretty soon he'll be all right. Will you stay and take care of him?"

"I stay. Where you go now?"

"Quien sabe?" muttered Johnny.

"Yeah; who knows?" echoed Brick. "Let's go. Better take rifles and plenty shells, pardner; we may need 'em."

They saddled their horses and rode away from the rancho.

"No use goin' to Sicomoro," said Johnny wearily. "The officers can't do a thing. They'd eventually get a company of soldiers to camp down here, but what good does that do us?"

"I reckon it's a two-handed job," said Brick. "We're a couple of danged fools to go hornin' around down in that country. I've got a redhead to alibi my foolishness, but you ain't got a thing."

"You think not?" softly. "My God, man, my alibi is somewhere down there right now."

"That's right; I forgot."

It did not take Silent long to ride back to Gomez Springs. Kelsey was not at the stable when he put up his horse, and he noticed that Breen's horse was not in its stall. Silent fed his horse, and then went around to the cantina. He saw Mahan standing in the doorway of a little tobacco shop across the street; so he went over to see him, wondering if Breen had noted his absence.

"Got back, eh?" grunted Mahan. "Yo're lucky, Slade."

223

"Lucky—why?"

Mahan laughed shortly and drew Silent away from the doorway.

"Don't never trust Kelsey," he said. "He told Breen what you told him. I heard a little of it, and after Kelsey got a few more drinks, he told me the rest. Breen went to Sicomoro to tell the sheriff where to pick you up. That's why I was surprised to see yuh."

"Kelsey told Breen, and Breen told the sheriff, eh?"

"Sure. Damn double-crossers. But Breen hates that redhead, and he knew you went to warn the redhead against Breen. Watch out for Breen now. He ain't back yet."

Silent lived up to his nickname for several moments. Then:

"Mahan, I'm goin' to have to kill Breen, I suppose."

"Looks thataway. There's some things yuh can't dodge. It's you or him. Things are gettin' tight down here. Breen has lost his grip. Too much tequila and too many of them damned doped cigarettes. Don't take a chance on him, Slade. He won't shoot square."

"And we ain't been paid yet," grinned Silent.

"Try and collect it."

"Well, I reckon I'm about to sever connections with Mr. Breen."

"I've got a little scheme, Slade. Want in on it?"

"I might be open to suggestions—if I live long enough."

"I talked with Lee Duck to-night. That Chink is smart. He's sick and tired of Breen. Yuh know what he thinks? He thinks Breen got all them diamonds. I asked him if he thought Breen had them in his safe in the cantina, and he said he didn't. I'll betcha that slant-eyed person has seen the inside of that safe. He thinks Breen has the diamonds cached at the rancho. If he's right, there's a lot of money that me and you might as well have."

"Sounds good," mused Silent. "But what about Lobo Gomez?"

"Let him in on it, or—"

"Would he double-cross Breen?"

"Lobo Gomez would double-cross his own mother for a lead peso. We'll go out and talk with Lobo. Let him send a man in for Breen, sabe? Once we get Breen out there, we'll make him talk. Lobo knows how. When the Lord made him, He forgot to stick a conscience into him. I reckon he's just as well off, as long as he keeps at his present occupation."

"Then I better keep away from Breen here in town. How about lettin' some of the boys in on the deal?"

"Yo're the only one I'd trust, Slade."

"Thanks. We better pull out before Breen gets back. He's prob'ly up in Sicomoro, waitin' for the sheriff to lead me in on a rope. The funny part of it was, that sheriff almost got me. I'm still full of rose thorns, when I fell back in the bushes."

"You probably got off lucky. Let's start travelin'."

They crossed the street and went around behind the cantina, where the horses were kept in a long adobe stable. Somebody had lighted the lantern, and as they came in Kelsey stepped out of a stall. His jaw sagged when he saw Silent, but before he could move the big cowboy had grabbed him and deftly removed the gun from his holster.

"Damn you!" snapped Kelsey, and drove his right fist against the side of Silent's neck with every ounce of power he owned. It might have sent an ordinary man reeling, but it had no effect on Slade.

Sock! Silent's left fist, traveling about eighteen inches, caught Kelsey flush on the chin. A slight hunch of the left shoulder, a pivot of the hips sent the punch home with worlds of power behind it; and Kelsey dropped like a pole-axed steer.

Silent said nothing. He removed Kelsey's belt and buckled it around his own waist.

"Gives me an extra gun," he said, and lifted his saddle off its peg against the wall.

"Great lovely dove!" blurted Mahan. "I've seen a lot of one-punch fights, but I never—man, you shore buttoned up his mind for him!"

"He deserved a good slap," grunted Silent. "If I ever get a crack at Breen—I'll *hit* him."

"I dunno," said Mahan, as he tightened his cinch.

"Dunno what?" queried Silent.

"Dunno why you pack a gun; you don't need it."

CHAPTER XIV

BREEN'S RANCHO

THE wind was hissing through the mesquite and sage when Breen and his four captors swung off the dry-wash on the trail to the rancho. The moon had been blotted out by the clouds, and a distant rumble of thunder presaged a storm. As they drew in sight of the house, Breen breathed a sigh of relief. There was no light showing at the rancho.

But Ed Pico was no fool. He halted the cavalcade two hundred yards from the ranch-house and sent Al Abelardo ahead to reconnoiter. Breen grinned to himself. Gomez had a couple of Yaqui Indians doing guard duty, and they would probably let Al do his spying, in order to capture all of them. Breen had no doubt that the Yaqui knew of their approach.

It was fifteen minutes before Al came back and reported the ranch-house deserted. Breen almost laughed aloud, as they went forward, but his laugh turned to consternation, when Ed Pico and Bill Abelardo came from the house and began taking off the ropes.

"Nobody home, except the Chinese cook, and he's now roped to a chair," said Pico. "Climb down, Breen."

Breen dismounted slowly, his mind in a whirl, and preceded Pico into the house, where he saw the Chinese cook tied to a chair and Al Abelardo building a fire in the fireplace. Breen sat down in a chair, and Bill Abelardo quickly roped him tight.

The wind blew down the old flue, sending a shower of ashes across the hard-packed adobe floor.

"A good night to be under a roof," smiled Ed Pico, rubbing his hands. He turned to Breen. "Where are the diamonds?"

Breen stared at the fire, his lips closed tightly. For once in his life he was up against a hard deal, and he didn't know how to get out of it.

"Plenty of time to get the diamonds," he said slowly. "You can't go back until the storm is over."

Ed Pico laughed at him. "No? You're wrong. Give me the diamonds, and see what I care for a little storm. You think to gain time, eh? Perhaps, if we stay here long enough, some of your men will surprise us. Is that the idea? Just rest your mind on that score, Breen; we are not going to stay long. Tell us where the diamonds are."

"Suppose," said Breen thoughtfully, "that I refuse."

"We thought of that," said Joe Pico quickly. He walked over to the fire of mesquite roots, and lifted the handle of an old branding-iron, the brand end of which was already in the flames. It was a queer-shaped Mexican brand, which would cover at least six inches square. Breen flinched.

"It will soon be hot," said Joe. "This old iron heats quickly."

"Bluffing, eh?" grunted Breen.

"Why bluff?" asked Ed Pico. "Your hide means nothing to us."

"Suppose I don't even know where the diamonds are hidden?"

"You are supposing a lot for a man in your position."

Breen knew that Ed Pico was not bluffing. He held the whiphand, and he was going to use it. But where was Gomez, he wondered? Why had he left the rancho? Had he decided to raid the Rancho del Rosa that night, or had he and his men gone to Gomez Springs? The Chinaman would know; but Breen was afraid to ask him for fear Pico might hurry the issue. The Chinaman sat there, gazing blankly at the flames. It was immaterial to him who was in charge, as long as they did no worse than to rope him to a chair.

Joe Pico tested the iron against a piece of mesquite-root, and a curl of smoke twisted upward from the contact.

"I guess it is hot enough," he said. "Don't want it to sear too quick."

At a sign from Ed Pico, the Abelardo brothers unroped Breen from the chair, shoved him over to a rough bench, where they flung him on his face and began roping him down. Breen cursed them bitterly, but they only grinned. This was work to their liking.

Ed Pico twisted an old rag around the handle of the iron and came over to Breen.

"Shall I remove his shirt?" asked Joe.

"No need of it," replied Ed. "This will remove cloth as well as hide. Now, Breen, talk quickly. I will give you ten seconds to tell where the diamonds are located. Feel the warmth of the iron?"

He held it close to Breen's back, and Breen flinched.

"They are buried under the fireplace," he said.

Ed Pico laughed and flung the iron aside.

"I thought a little heat would make you talk. Find a pick or a bar of some kind, Joe. If he has lied to us, he will get at least one brand, before he gets a chance to lie again."

Joe found a short piece of drill steel in the kitchen, which he brought in, along with a bucket of water. They extinguished the flames, and waited for the ashes to cease steaming. It was raining now, and the drops came hissing down the old flue. A flash of lightning illuminated the room brightly, followed quickly by a crash of thunder.

Ed Pico raked the ashes out across the hearth and attacked the heat-hardened bottom of the fireplace, which was as hard as pottery. Joe held the lamp, while the Abelardos squatted at the corners, watching the operation closely.

"He lies," said Joe softly. "That has never been disturbed. See, it is as hard as stone."

"It would harden quickly, if put back wet," grunted Ed. "See if there is not a pick around here. Madre de Dios!"

Ed had turned his head and looked back at Breen. Just inside the doorway stood Lobo Gomez, water streaming off his huge sombrero, while behind him stood two of his men; and each man was covering the group at the fireplace with rifles.

The four men got up slowly. Lobo's white teeth gleamed beneath the black of his mustache, which was also dripping wet.

"Do not move," warned Lobo. "Their guns, Juan."

One man came forward and collected all the guns, taking them back to Gomez, who motioned him to the kitchen with them, and then came forward a few paces. The man came back from the kitchen and Gomez sent him to get ropes. Breen laughed triumphantly, while Gomez's two men proceeded to rope the four men tightly, sitting them against the wall.

"They threatened to brand me," said Breen, when one of the men removed his ropes. Hc sat up and rubbed his arms violently, while Gomez went over and inspected the fireplace.

"What were you looking for?" he asked Ed Pico.

"Ask Breen, he knows."

Breen laughed shortly. "They captured me in Sicomoro. Thought I knew where the diamonds were; so I lied. I needed time for you to come back. Where in the devil have you been?"

Gomez grinned widely and spoke to one of the men, who went out into the storm. Gomez kicked the charred sticks back into the fireplace, put dry wood on, and told his other man to rebuild the fire.

"I have been very busy," said Gomez expansively. "You shall see what I have been doing. Behold!"

With a dramatic gesture he pointed toward the doorway.

First came Robert Maxwell, hatless, coatless, soaked to the skin, his hands tied behind him. His lips were bleeding from a blow in the mouth. Behind him came Marie and Juanita, white-faced, dripping. Neither of them wore coat or hat. Behind them stumbled Buck Eads and Leo Herrera, their arms tightly roped to their sides. Then came the rest of Gomez's army, eight Mexicans and a couple of half-clad Yaqui Indians.

Buck's right eye was swollen shut, and Leo was bleeding from a cut on his cheek. Taking them all in all, they were a helpless, bedraggled lot of people. Breen stared at them foolishly, checking them over. This was more than he had bargained for. Breen wet his dry lips and continued to stare.

Ed Pico laughed outright at the expression on Breen's face, and Breen whirled on him like a tiger.

"Shut up!" he snapped.

"A fine mess," said Pico slowly, ignoring Breen's order. "You'll pay for this, Breen."

Breen struck him across the mouth, knocking Pico against the wall.

"You won't see the payment made," growled Breen angrily.

"What is the meaning of this, Breen?" asked Maxwell. "Did you send these men to raid my rancho?"

"That is my business," growled Breen. He went closer and looked at Marie, but she looked back at him defiantly. Then he stepped over and faced Juanita.

"So you are Scotty McKee's daughter, eh? I knew him well. By God, you're a pretty girl."

He turned to Gomez. "You didn't do so badly, after all."

"I am Gomez."

"But you didn't get the one I wanted."

"He was not there. One man offered fight, and Felipe broke his head with a rifle barrel. For that, Felipe gets a bottle of tequila, eh?"

Breen scowled, but nodded. Gomez had gone

too far, but that could not be helped now. Breen would have willingly traded them all for Brick Davidson, and thrown in the Picos and Abelardos for good measure. He turned to Gomez, who was unroping the Chinaman.

"Where was the redhead?" he asked.

Gomez shrugged his heavy shoulders. "Who knows? These cattle will not tell."

Gomez spoke in Spanish, but they could all understand it.

"Who's cattle, you bat-eared pig?" asked Buck Eads. "Take these ropes off, and I'll fight the whole gang of you."

"When we take the ropes off—you won't know it," said Breen.

"Don't let them bluff you," advised Ed Pico. "Breen is a bag of dirty wind."

"What are you doin' over here?" asked Buck.

Ed Pico grinned sourly, but did not reply.

"He made a mistake," growled Breen, and quickly added, "And it is a mistake for which he will pay well. Sit down along the wall, you folks. Take it easy while you can. Gomez, instruct that Chinaman to cook a lot of food. Open up some tequila. You'll find a case or two hidden in some baled-hay in the stable. Give the men a drink—our men, of course."

"Breen," said Maxwell calmly, "you better turn us all loose. You are mad to do a thing like this. Correct this mistake before it is too late."

"Mad, eh? You think so, do you? I suppose you were not mad when you stole those diamonds, eh? You'll tell where they are, before I get through with you."

"You crazy fool, I never saw the diamonds. At least, send the women back home. They have no part in this."

"You think I will? Do I look like a fool, Maxwell? I'm boss down here, and by the time there is any investigation, I will be a long ways from here. And as for the women—" Breen laughed shortly. "All is fair in love and war, remember. My only regret is that we haven't the redhead with us to-night."

"He will kill you for this," said Marie evenly.

"Will he? My dear, I am not afraid of your precious redhead."

"Yo're a liar!" snorted Buck Eads in English. "You swallered crooked when his name was mentioned. I dunno what it's all about, but my money is on the sorrel-top to win."

"My bet rides with yours," said Ed Pico.

"He's toff bebby," said Bill Abelardo, airing his English.

"Shut off," advised Al. "You get your face in tro'ble."

"Go ahead and have your say," advised Breen. "Words are nothing. You will quit talking when I give the word. Put the bottles on the table, Gomez."

He yanked the cork from a bottle and held it up.

"Good luck to you," he said sarcastically. "You'll need it before the night is over."

He drank heavily, while the Mexicans grabbed for bottles, knocking the necks off against the table. A corkscrew meant nothing to them.

"Before you get too drunk, stop and realize what this means," advised Maxwell.

"I never get too drunk to run my own business."

"What's all this about you having the diamonds, Maxwell?" asked Ed Pico.

"That is one of Breen's insane theories."

Breen laughed and took another drink.

"Funny, isn't it? Pico thought I had them. He captured me in Sicomoro, intending to force a confession from me. I told him they were here at the rancho; so he brought me here. He was going to use a hot branding-iron on my skin, if I didn't tell him where they were. The fool was going to turn me over to the sheriff on a murder charge; so I lied about the diamonds to get back here. You can see what happened to Mr. Pico."

"What murder was that—Dell Harper?" asked Buck Eads.

"No—a fellow named Sohmes."

"Did you kill Sohmes?" asked Maxwell.

"Pico says I did. What's the difference?"

Breen and Gomez sat down in a corner of the room, each with a bottle of tequila, while they talked in low tones. The two girls were badly frightened. Gomez's little army paid no attention to the captives. It was of little interest to them, as long as they had food and drink.

Out in the kitchen the Chinaman rattled pans and pots, as he cooked their meal.

"What are we going to do?" whispered Juanita.

"What can we do?" queried Marie.

"Keep yore nerve," advised Buck. "If they get drunk enough, we might have a chance. I'd give four bits for a cigarette."

"I'd give everythin' I've got for a six-gun, long enough to shoot twice," said Leo Herrera, eyeing Breen and Gomez.

It was raining hard now, and they could hear the water running off the eaves. The room began to get smoky from the kitchen fireplace, mingled with the smoke of broiling meats. Breen and Gomez finished their bottles, and a Mexican brought them two more.

"Go to it!" grunted Buck. "That stuff will get 'em, if they take plenty."

The Chinaman came in and placed tin dishes on the table. He grinned wickedly at Ed Pico, who flung out a foot and tripped the Chinaman. It amused the Mexicans, but it made Breen mad.

"One more move like that, and I'll drill you full of holes," he said.

Ed Pico laughed up at him, drew up his foot, as though to kick Breen, but Breen sprang back and ordered two of the Mexicans to rope Pico's legs.

As Breen started to walk back to where Gomez sat, he stopped suddenly. Above the noise of the storm came the unmistakable sound of a shot, followed quickly by two more. Gomez sprang to his feet.

"You had guards out?" snapped Breen.

"My two Yaquis—yes."

Came the pounding of a running horse, which jerked up at the door. Gomez flung the door open, and a man fell inside. Breen stepped aside and let the man fall, covering him with a gun. It was Kelsey. He tried to sit up, but sprawled backwards on the floor.

"What's wrong with you?" asked Breen savagely.

"He's been shot," said Gomez.

Kelsey's face was white, as he stared around.

"Shot?" he said vacantly. "Oh, yes. Is Slade and Mahan here?"

"They're in—what do you mean?" asked Breen anxiously. "What about Slade? Did he come back?"

Kelsey nodded weakly. "Came back. Jumped me in the stable—knocked me out. Going to get you, I think—came ahead of me. Somebody shot me out there."

"They never came here," said Breen. "Did Slade know I sent the sheriff after him?"

"Maybe Mahan—told him. Who—shot—me, Breen?"

He stared at Breen, his mouth sagging, as though waiting for the answer. Then he sagged back to the floor.

"Put him in the stable," said Breen callously. "Your Yaquis are efficient, Lobo."

Two of the men picked him up and went out through the kitchen.

"They're breakin' bad for yuh, Breen," said Buck ominously.

"One more remark like that, and you'll follow Kelsey."

Buck blinked, but said nothing more. Breen was drunk enough to make good his threat.

Silent and Mahan had no idea that Breen would be at the rancho. As far as they knew, Breen was still in Sicomoro, or on his way back to Gomez Springs. They were having a difficult time in keeping their horses on the old trail, because the horses did not like to face the storm.

They were nearing the ranch-house, and had lost the trail for a few minutes, when a flash of lightning showed a rider galloping on the trail past them. The flash was so brief that they were unable to distinguish the horse or rider, but a few moments later they saw the flash of a rifle. Came two more flashes, the reports close together.

Silent and Mahan drew up their horses close together, wondering what it was all about. It was not long until they saw the glow of light, when Kelsey fell through the ranch-house door.

Mahan led the way, and they circled far to the left, coming in at the rear of the old stable, where they dismounted. It was raining hard, and both men were soaked to the skin.

"What was the meanin' of them shots?" queried Silent.

Mahan laughed softly. "Lobo Gomez must have posted guards. It was a lucky thing that rider came past ahead of us. Wonder who he is, and what's goin' on at the house. Did you get a look at that horse?"

"Looked black to me."

"Kelsey rides a black. By golly, it might have been Kelsey. It would be just like him to ride out here to warn Breen. He'd know now that you and Breen would come to a showdown, and he might have taken a chance that Breen came here, instead of going back to town."

They worked along the stable until they were near one of the doors, and heard voices near the back door of the house. The two Mexicans were bringing the body of Kelsey out to the stable. Silent and Mahan crouched against the wall, while the two men and their burden went into the stable. They came out in a few moments and went to the house.

"They were carryin' somethin'," said Silent. "Didn't yuh hear 'em gruntin'?"

"Let's take a look."

They slipped inside the stable, warm with the odors of horses. Silent lighted a match and looked around. Every stall contained a horse, except the first one, which was used as storage. Here a pair of boots were in evidence, sticking out from beneath an old blanket. Silent lighted another match, while Mahan removed the blanket.

"It was Kelsey," he said softly. "Dead as a doorknob."

He threw back the blanket, and they went to the doorway.

"Kelsey got what we'd have got, if we had been first," said Mahan. "Lobo must have posted his two Yaquis out there, and I've seen 'em hit hawks on the wing with their old Mausers."

"Why would Gomez have guards out?" asked Silent. "Who is he afraid of? Looks kinda funny to me—and on a night like this."

"It is kinda funny. I never thought of that. He wouldn't post 'em against Breen or Breen's gang; and who else would he expect?"

Silent went back, lighted a few more matches, and looked at the horses. He came back to the doorway, where Mahan was watching the house.

"Them broncs has been rode hard to-night, Mahan. They ain't through steamin' yet. Gomez and his men have been for a ride."

"Mebby they went over to capture yore red-headed friend."

"No, I don't believe that."

"You don't know Lobo Gomez."

"I suppose not, but I know he wouldn't hesitate to cross the Border at night. But if he went to-night, Breen didn't know it, 'cause he sent the sheriff after me. He wouldn't want the sheriff at the Maxwell ranch, if he knew Gomez was to be there."

"That might be true; but when it comes to devilment, Gomez would pick his own sweet time."

"I guess that's right; he's bull-headed enough, that's a cinch. Our trouble is to find out what happened and who is in there. If Kelsey lived long enough, he told Breen what happened in town. Breen will be on the lookout for both of us, and if he and Lobo catch us, we'll be strung out alongside of Kelsey."

"Our best bet is to take it slow and easy. If another man comes out here, we'll both hop him, stick a gun under his chin and make him tell us the story. We won't dare investigate the house. It's so damn dark right now that you couldn't see a man six feet away."

"Anyway it's warm and dry in here," laughed Silent. "We'll wait a while and see what happens."

CHAPTER XV

BRICK ON THE PROD

BRICK and Johnny missed the trail, where it crossed the dry-wash, and were out there, wandering around like a pair of lost geese in the storm. Neither of them were dressed for wet weather, and they were sodden and discouraged by the time they found the trail which led to Breen's rancho.

Brick was cautious. He knew just how far it was from the edge of the dry-wash to the rancho, and he had a feeling that, if the raiders had gone to the rancho, they would post a guard on the trail. Johnny was anxious to investigate the rancho, and wanted to ride right in, but Brick told him he was a fool.

"You won't be any good to 'em dead, Johnny. They may not be at the ranch, but we'll play that they are and do a little Injun actin'."

The wind made plenty of noise; so there was little danger of any one hearing them, but it was also so dark that they couldn't see ahead for any distance. Brick led the way, his horse at a slow walk.

He knew they were nearing the rancho. Suddenly he stopped his horse. Not over fifty feet ahead some one had scratched a match. And through the drifting rain he saw the shadowy figures of the two Yaqui Indians, lighting their cigarettes. They were apparently crouched against a small mesquite near the trail, with a blanket half over the both of them to break the force of the wind and rain.

Brick dismounted quickly and Johnny piled off after him. They let the two horses turn their rumps to the storm, knowing that they were both rein-broke and would stand there for hours.

Brick whispered what he had seen to Johnny, who crouched beside him. Then they saw the flicker of a lighted cigarette. Humped over, half-crawling, they circled the two men. Brick was filled with the lust of battle just now. They could have avoided the two Yaquis and gone on to the rancho, but both men, in range parlance, were on the prod.

The two Indians were unconscious of their presence. They were there to try and prevent any one from coming in over that trail. They had shot at one man who ignored their hail. It was uncomfortable out there, and they huddled together under the old blanket, smoking, talking in a mixture of Yaqui and Spanish, wishing Gomez had been thoughtful enough to have furnished them with a bottle of tequila.

They had just agreed that the blanket was inadequate protection, when the top of the world seemed to crash down upon them. Came a flurry of arms and legs, the dull *sug, sug, sug* of flailing six-shooters—silence.

"How'd yuh comin', Johnny?"

"She's fine with me, pardner. Tore hell out of my shirt on that darn mesquite. Tried to fall on the end of that cigarette, and there was a limb between me and the light. I'm settin' on mine."

"Roll him over here to me, and then get some ropes."

Brick sat on both of them, while Johnny brought up the horses and produced the ropes. Neither of the Indians was interested in the proceeding, although neither of them was seriously disabled. Brick roped them together, threw their guns away, stacked them up against the mesquite and covered them with the old blanket.

"The trail is now open," said Brick. "In case we want to make a quick getaway, we won't have anybody shootin' at the west end of us as we go east."

"Them Injuns will shore have somethin' to write on the rocks," laughed Johnny, as they mounted. "I don't reckon there's any more guards scattered around."

"And don't never let anybody tell yuh that cigarettes ain't injurious. If them Injuns hadn't learned to smoke, we wouldn't have seen 'em. They can blame cigarettes for their downfall."

Brick led the way off the trail. He had a good idea of location, and wanted to approach the house from the rear. Their horses stopped against the corral fence, where they dismounted, circled the fence, and came in behind the stable. They discovered the two saddled horses, but had no idea who owned them.

Brick climbed through the corral fence, where he found more horses, all saddled. He went back to Johnny, and they moved their horses back to the side of the corral, where they had first stopped. Brick whispered the news to Johnny.

"They're all here, I'll betcha," said Johnny. "Let's see what we can find in the stable."

Back around the fence they went, past the two horses huddled in against the end of the long stable, and felt their way along the wall to the door, which they found unlocked. They listened for a while, but heard nothing except the drip, drip of the eaves.

Brick shoved the door open and stepped inside, followed closely by Johnny. It was as dark as the proverbial black cat in there; so dark that the outdoors seemed light in comparison. The door sagged shut behind them, and as Brick fumbled for a match something crashed into him and he went backwards, clutched in a vise-like grip.

He thought he heard Johnny cry out, and then they hit the packed earth of the stable. As far as Brick was concerned, the surprise and shock only lasted a second, and he was fighting when he hit the floor. He was as hard as nails and as wiry as a cat. The shock of the fall loosened the grip around his right arm, which he started working like a piston, throwing short-arm punches into whatever or whoever might be trying to hug him.

This certain party was not partial to such treatment, and in trying to control that flying fist, relaxed on the left, which took up the burden. There was no noise, except animal-like grunts, thudding of feet, the ripping of wet cloth. Brick hadn't been hurt yet.

He fought so fast that he finally broke the hold of the other man, twisted sideways on one shoulder, whirled over on his hands and knees, and filled his lungs with air. His gun had fallen from its holster. Anyway, he didn't want to use the gun for fear of hitting Johnny.

He got cautiously to his feet, hunched forward, fists doubled, when a clutching hand brushed his arm. Quickly he stepped in and swung a right-hand smash, guessing distance and direction. His fist smashed solidly against cloth, and a man grunted.

Before Brick could recover his balance a blow caught him in the shoulder, almost knocking him off his feet. He went backwards, caught his heel, and sat down heavily. That punch hurt him. His right arm seemed paralyzed for a few moments. It was like the kick of a horse.

"Damn yuh, lay still!" panted a voice. "I'll

twist yore arm off, if yuh don't quit it. Kick me in the face, will yuh!"

"Look out, Mahan; I didn't get the other one."

"You did, but yuh don't know it, Silent," said Brick breathlessly.

"Eh?" grunted Silent. "Brick, is that you? You danged—"

"Go ahead and chide me," said Brick. "You big bull, yuh almost broke my shoulder."

"What's all this about?" asked Mahan.

"Keep yore big fist out of my mouth!" gritted Johnny. "I'll bite yore fingers off, if yuh do that again. Brick, are yuh hurt?"

Silent lighted a match and looked around. Mahan was on his knees, straddling Johnny Snow, while Brick sat in the first stall, beside Kelsey's feet, a blank expression in his face.

"Mahan, meet Brick Davidson," said Silent.

"Glad t' meetcha," nodded Mahan. "Kinda wet evenin', ain't it?"

Mahan's nose was bleeding and his upper lip was swelling.

"It shore is wet," agreed Brick. "Yuh might set on somethin' besides my pardner, Mr. Mahan."

"He's a damn little buzz-saw," said Mahan. "We thought you was a couple Mexicans. I choosed me this one in the dark, and I didn't much more than git ahold of him, when I says to myself, 'Mahan, if this here is a Mexican, whatsa use of 'em bein' a downtrodden people?'"

249

"But how come you to be here, Brick?" asked Silent, as he lighted more matches.

Brick recovered his six-shooter and leaned against the wall, while Johnny Snow got to his feet and brushed the dirt out of his eyes. It did not take Brick long to tell what had happened at the Rancho del Rosa. Silent took a chance and lighted the dirty old lantern, after shutting the door tightly.

Silent wanted to go right to the house and start a battle.

"Do yuh think I'm goin' to stand for that dirty crew pawin' over them girls?" he demanded.

"I'll go with yuh," offered Johnny anxiously.

"And get both of yuh killed off," said Mahan. "That would only leave two of us to do the job right—and that ain't enough."

Brick eyed the legs and feet of the first casualty.

"That's Kelsey," explained Silent. "He was one of our gang, and he was the one who told Breen about me goin' to the Maxwell place. I reckon he was Breen's chief stool-pigeon. Anyway, he came ridin' hell-for-leather, and got shot on the wing by a couple of Gomez's guards. He got to the house before he died, I reckon; so they stacked him away out here."

"But how did you fellers get past them guards?" asked Mahan.

Brick explained what had happened and the two men seemed to enjoy it.

"You shore were lucky," declared Mahan. "I figure that Breen sent Gomez to capture you, and when Gomez didn't find you, he raided the whole danged outfit. Gomez ain't got no more conscience than a snake."

"Neither has Breen," said Silent.

"Not a trace. He's a white man gone bad. He's got to be bad, or lose out. No, I don't think Breen would stop at anythin'. That's why I'm worried about them girls."

"He'll probably burn Maxwell's feet, tryin' to force him to tell where he hid the diamonds," said Silent, "and if Maxwell don't know, or won't tell, yuh never know what Breen might do. I think I'll walk right in and kill Breen and Lopez. With them out of the way, we've got a chance."

"Sounds easy," said Johnny hopefully.

"Oh, shore," grunted Mahan sarcastically. "Don't be foolish. Breen is nobody's fool, and neither is Gomez. You'd never get in that house. If Kelsey lived long enough to talk, Breen will have the outside of the house plenty guarded. Them doors are six-inch oak and the walls are two feet thick. You'd never get in. They'd wait until daylight and then pick us off.

"There's only one way out, unless yuh want to head back into the hills. Gomez could cut us off too quick."

"Then what are we goin' to do?" asked Silent.

"Wait and see. Wait for a break."

251

"Wait!" snorted Johnny. "I didn't come over here to wait."

"I think Mahan's right," said Brick thoughtfully. "And another thing, I want Breen alive, if I can get him."

"Give me his ears," said Silent.

Things were going so peaceably in the ranchhouse. Gomez had drunk enough tequila to paralyze an ordinary man, but he didn't show it, except that he became more boastful and dangerous. Breen was drunk enough to conceive a great hate of the big outlaw. The Chinaman had piled a lot of smoking food on the table, and the men drew up their benches. Breen sat at one end of the table and Gomez at the other.

But Breen didn't eat. He had a bottle of liquor at his elbow, which he drank sparingly now, realizing that he couldn't afford to get too drunk. Gomez ate noisily, guzzling his food, keeping his pig-like eyes on Breen. The two girls huddled together, saying nothing. Maxwell sat against the wall, his back very straight, his face white in the lamplight.

Finally the big outlaw shoved his plate aside and lighted a cigarette. He looked over at the two girls and grinned widely. Breen scowled. It was the first time that Gomez had paid any attention to them.

"You like theese place?" he asked in English.

"Puerco!" said Juanita disgustedly.

Gomez stiffened suddenly, puffing his cheeks angrily. Ed Pico laughed out loud, but Gomez paid no attention to him.

"Puerco?" muttered Gomez. "So that is your opinion, Señorita?"

"Yes," she said bravely in Spanish. "Your ancestors were all pigs; scavenger pigs, living in filth."

Gomez got quickly to his feet, although a bit unsteady now. Breen also jumped up and stepped around the table.

"Stop it, Lobo," he said. "You would be a fool to expect a flattering opinion, after what you have done to-night. I will pay you well for it, because these prisoners belong to me—not to you."

"How much do you pay?"

"I promised a thousand pesos for the redhead. You failed to get him. These people I did not want. But it was not your fault; so I shall pay you the thousand pesos, and you will take your men back to town."

Gomez laughed nastily. "A thousand pesos? And I ride away with my men, while you force Maxwell to tell where the diamonds are. Is that your game, my friend? Do you think Gomez is a fool? I risked myself and my men to-night, and you offer a thousand pesos! You seek to use me as a tool, and then toss me aside. I am Gomez!"

He struck himself on the chest and glared at Breen.

"Sic 'm, Tige!" grunted Buck Eads. "Hop at him, Breen. I'd like to see you two cut-throats tie into each other."

Breen turned to one of the Mexicans. "Take a rag and gag that man."

The Mexican started to get up from the table, but Gomez motioned for him to stay seated.

"I order my own men," he told Breen.

"Do not let Breen boss things, Gomez!" said Buck, in Spanish.

"Gag me that man," ordered Gomez, and the Mexican got up from the table.

"What the hell?" grunted Buck wailingly. "Side in with 'em and get a dirty rag in the mouth."

The rest of the assemblage kept still now, as none of them cared for a gag. Breen laughed softly, but there was a worried expression on his face.

"How much do you demand, Gomez?" he asked.

The big outlaw laughed deep in his chest.

"A change of tune, eh? How much? You will force Maxwell to tell what he knows of the diamonds? Certainly? Well," he twisted his mustache thoughtfully, "I ask for one half of the diamonds, and my share of these," he gestured toward the prisoners.

"Your share of these?" queried Breen. "What do you mean?"

"What will you do with the women?"

Breen hesitated. That was something he had never planned. If any of them ever got back across the line, Breen would be damned in any country. Even Mexico would be too small for him.

He looked around the smoky room. Four men from Sicomoro, five people from the Rancho del Rosa. He could send them back safely, and perhaps nothing would ever come of it; that is, there would not be any hue and cry for his scalp. He could never go back across the Border. In fact, he would have to be further south in order to play safe. They knew he had hired Gomez to make the raid, and Gomez had said that one of the Maxwell cowboys had been killed.

The authorities would charge him with murder and raiding. It was not a pleasant outlook. If the Government knew of the raid, they would work through the Mexican Government to apprehend him. And he couldn't depend on all these folks keeping still. They might promise anything, in order to get away, but a forced promise is no promise at all.

But there was a spark of decency left in Breen's heart. It flared up for a moment and he turned to Gomez.

"The women go back," he said, but added

quickly, "as soon as we force Maxwell to tell where the diamonds are hidden."

"You fool!" said Maxwell coldly. "You know as well as I do that I have never seen the diamonds."

Gomez grinned, and turned to Ed Pico. There was no love lost between these two, and Pico scowled up at him.

"You came here to get the diamonds from Breen?" asked Gomez.

"He admitted hiding them here."

"You forced me to admit a lie," said Breen quickly.

"Where did you get your information?" asked Gomez.

Ed Pico shrugged his shoulders. "We have ways. It was said that Breen got the diamonds from Wong Kee, and then had Wong Kee murdered; so that nobody would know. Harper did not carry the diamonds, but he was killed for a purpose—to place the blame on some one else."

"On the hijackers?" asked Gomez.

"Perhaps. It would then appear that Harper had been murdered and the diamonds stolen from him."

Gomez went back to the table and took a drink from his bottle. He had never thought of the incident in this light.

"And then Breen murdered Sohmes," said Ed Pico.

Gomez grunted softly and looked at Breen. Gomez knew Sohmes.

"That is a lie," gritted Breen angrily. "Who ever started that tale?"

"It seems to be generally known," said Maxwell slowly. "Sohmes was at my rancho, from where he went to Gomez Springs, and never returned."

"How do you know this?" demanded Breen coldly.

"You might ask the officers that question. It is no affair of mine."

The spark of decency died out quickly. Breen laughed harshly and took another drink.

"Well, suppose I did kill him?" he snarled. "You can't prove it. Even if you could prove it, what good would it do you? Are you the judge and jury? The law is a long ways from here. I do as I please."

He walked over to Ed Pico. "You accuse me of murder, do you, Pico? Do you know any prayers, or shall I send for a priest? And you," speaking to Joe Pico, "what have you to say? And you, you damn Abelardos!"

"He's toff hombre, Beel," said Al. Bill nodded slowly.

"I tell you one time," said Bill slowly, "we mak' meestake from not keel heem biffore. He's toff jeeger, you bet."

"You'll think I'm a tough jigger, before I finish with you."

"I'm not scare from you," said Bill. "I'm jus' weesh for de radhad to come. Thees he's girl. Dios! He's get pretty damn mad, thees radhad."

Breen scowled down at Bill Abelardo.

"Which one is the redhead's girl?" he asked.

Bill shrugged his shoulders. "Quien sabe?"

"I think you lie, Abelardo."

"Bot you are not for sure, eh? Go 'head and mak' beeg meestake."

Breen walked back and sat down at the table, from where he studied the two girls. It seemed to amuse Gomez.

"I'd give ten thousand pesos to have the redhead here," he said to Gomez. "Ten thousand pesos in hard cash."

"Go get him, and pay the money to yourself," said Gomez. "I shall go cross the Border no more. When I have settled with you, I shall go to Mexico City and live like a gentleman."

"And get hung," growled Breen.

Gomez laughed drunkenly. "With money? Bah! I have never been a political; never took sides. What does Mexico City know about what is done up in this country?"

"How much money do you expect to get from me?"

"Sufficient for my needs. Perhaps you will need to go with me, eh? Let's have another bottle and come to a settlement."

Breen nodded and reached for a bottle.

"Plenty of time to talk about a settlement," he said. "The night is young. Perhaps we can make a deal between us."

He took a long drink, and leaned across the table toward Gomez.

"It is really too bad that this house will not burn," he said.

"Burn?" Gomez wiped his dripping mustache with the back of his hand.

"Fire wipes out many things."

Gomez grinned and took another drink. He was not so dense that he did not get the significance of the remark.

"When do you send the women back home?" asked Maxwell.

Breen laughed and shook his head. "We are not concerned with time down here."

"Don't be a fool, Breen. Remember you are a white man, an American; not a savage. I can forgive you many things, if you send them safely home."

"Even to telling where you hid the diamonds?"

"I tell you, I have never seen the diamonds."

"They go back, when you tell. Don't hurry. Think it over a while."

Gomez leered at the girls, and finally got up and went over to them. He yanked Juanita to her feet and led her over to the table.

"Sit down," he ordered, shoving her against the bench.

"What do you think you are doing?" asked Breen angrily.

"Observe closely," retorted Gomez, as he took the ropes off Juanita.

"Don't be a fool."

Gomez laughed harshly and patted Juanita on the shoulder.

"Why keep ropes on a dove, eh?" he laughed. "Have a drink?"

Juanita rubbed her sore wrists, paying no attention to Gomez. He grasped her by the shoulder and roughly forced her to face him.

"You impossible brute!" she said wearily.

Gomez grinned in her face. "You are not afraid of me, eh? Good! I like a woman who is not afraid of me. So you are the daughter of McKee."

"Did you know my father?" she asked.

"Almost too well," laughed Gomez. "Ask our scowling friend at the other end of the table. He is drunk. But do not be afraid. There is not enough tequila in the world to make Gomez drunk. We are safe. Two Yaqui guarding the trail, a man at the front and one at the rear of the house. Our scowling friend fears the redhead."

Gomez threw back his big head and laughed heartily.

"It is a good joke. He will pay me much money very soon. How would you like to go to Mexico City with me?"

"Don't be a fool," growled Breen. "I will pay

260

you what you ask, except that there are no diamonds to divide. If I give you ten thousand pesos, will you take your men and leave this rancho?"

"So you have ten thousand pesos, eh?"

Breen bit his lip and ignored the question.

Gomez laughed, got to his feet, and began pacing the floor. He was none too secure on his feet. Every eye in the room was upon him. He stopped in front of Ed Pico.

"You have said your prayers?" he asked. "Or are you waiting for our friend Breen to send for a priest? I believe he mentioned it."

"He whined like a puppy, when he saw the hot iron," said Pico.

Gomez laughed drunkenly, nodding slowly. Breen got to his feet and came toward Pico, gripping a tequila bottle in his right hand, but the big outlaw stepped in front of him.

"Go and sit down," ordered Gomez. "I am in charge here, and my orders will be obeyed."

Breen moved back, realizing that he was little better off than the prisoners. Gomez whispered to Felipe, who seemed to be his lieutenant, and the little, thin-faced Mexican nodded quickly. Breen turned his head slowly, and saw two of the rifle-barrels carelessly pointed in his direction. Gomez could have disarmed Breen, but he probably chose to let Breen know that his gun would do him little good.

Gomez sat down again and looked at Juanita.

"I think I will marry you," he said. "Of these people," he swept a big hand in a gesture of contempt, "I have no concern. We will take payment from Breen, turn these people loose, and get married in Gomez Springs, before we ride south with my men. How is that?"

"You drunken fool!" snorted Breen. "By this time there are men in Gomez Springs who would kill you on sight. Marry her? She does not wish to marry you, and what priest would marry her to you, if she objected? You have the brain of a pig."

Gomez laughed at Breen. "You think not, eh? Perhaps you want her. You would send for a priest to pray for Pico, before you killed him, eh? And all I ask is an honorable marriage. Brain of a pig, eh? See what you pay, before I am through with you."

"I would not marry you," said Juanita firmly. "Breen is right—no priest would marry me to you. Let us all go home. There are plenty of girls in Mexico."

"That's right," agreed Breen.

Gomez scowled at Breen for several moments, but grinned widely, when an idea struck him.

"This is good. I shall take this girl, priest or no priest. Then I shall turn all these folks loose, and let them take you across the Border. In that way you will not have long to worry about the payment you make to me. In that way, I shall atone for what I have done.

"What you say about the priest is true. No priest—" he stopped and stared at Juanita, who was looking at him, white-faced, her hands clenched in her lap.

"Madre de Dios!" he exclaimed. "Felipe! Go and get Padre Demente!"

"Padre Demente?" Felipe got slowly to his feet, staring at Gomez.

Padre Demente, the mad priest, lived alone in a tiny hut on the edge of the old dry-wash. Felipe knew him well, a weird figure of a man, who kept his face from the sight of man, dressed in rags, his head and face concealed in an old gunny sack.

"But the padre is mad," faltered Felipe. "He would not come. Seldom will he speak."

"Tell him it is a case of death," laughed Gomez. "No padre will refuse."

"Perhaps he is dead. I have not seen him for weeks."

"Go and get him!" roared Gomez, and Felipe went meekly out, speaking to the guard outside. Gomez turned to Juanita.

"This priest will marry us to-night. Take your choice between going with me as my wife, or not. But when we are married, I shall send all these folks back to their homes. Otherwise—" he shrugged his shoulders and opened a fresh bottle.

"I will marry you," said Juanita wearily.

"Good! Juan! Go out and tell the Yaqui guards that Felipe rides for a priest, and that he will be back."

Juan, short and squat, slightly unsteady, handed his rifle to another man, and went stumbling out through the front door. Breen studied Gomez through blood-shot eyes. He realized that Gomez was perfectly capable of doing just what he had said, and Breen had no relish to be turned over to Maxwell and the Pico brothers. A rope dangled before his eyes, and just now he could not see any way out.

"We might make it a double wedding," he suggested. "And the four of us could go to Mexico City."

Gomez laughed at the idea, but made no comment.

"You'd be a fool to take any chances with Breen," said Ed Pico, who could see Breen tampering with their chances for a safe return home.

"When he tells me where the diamonds are," said Gomez meaningly, "I might trade with him. What are diamonds to a man's life?"

"I haven't any diamonds."

"I think," said Gomez slowly, "there will be one marriage."

He turned his head and looked back at Ed Pico, when Breen surged to his feet and flung his tequila bottle. It was a sudden flash of intelligence on Breen's part. Felipe and Juan, the only two men of Gomez's crowd whom Gomez could depend upon, were out of the house.

The heavy bottle struck Gomez above the left ear, and the big outlaw fell sideways out of his seat. Breen's gun was out, swinging from side to side, covering the rest of Gomez's men, but they did not move. Dull-minded beasts, at best, they blinked at Breen, as he stepped around the table.

Gomez had been knocked cold, sprawling flat on his face. Breen tied his hands behind his back, took away his gun, and dragged him against the wall. Not a word had been said by any one. Breen stepped back to the table, as the door opened and Juan came in. Quickly the squat Mexican glanced around the room and saw his former master, half-lying against the wall, his head sagging on his chest.

"I am in charge here, Juan," said Breen.

Juan nodded shortly. He had found the two Yaqui guards roped together beside the trail and was anxious to tell Gomez about it, but Gomez was no longer in command.

"You told the guards?" asked Breen, lighting a cigarette with his left hand, while his right held a revolver below the top of the table.

"Si," nodded Juan.

"Sit down against the wall over there,"

pointing to a space beside Maxwell. "Gomez is no longer in charge here, and it will pay you to be loyal to me. I will not forget it."

"Esta buena," replied Juan, and sat down.

"Now," said Breen triumphantly, "the wheel of fortune has turned to my number—and I win. Let this crazy padre come. You will all be witnesses to a marriage, if this crazy fool is able to perform one. Juan, how far will Felipe have to go to find this Padre Demente?"

"Who knows? Perhaps two miles, if the padre is at his home. He wanders at times, and who knows where he may be found?"

Breen looked at Marie, his lips twisted in a sneer.

"You better pray that he is not wandering," said Breen meaningly.

The room was silent for several moments. The Chinaman brought in more dry mesquite roots, which he piled on the fire, shuffling back to his place in the kitchen. Breen went over and looked at the heavy bar across the front door.

"Breen," said Maxwell, "you can't go through with this. Just stop and realize what it means. Play square with your own soul for a few moments, and you will realize what a terrible thing you are doing."

Breen laughed harshly. "Soul! What is a soul? You think I'm at the end of my string, eh? Well, what if I am? I'll play to the last card."

"But what have we ever done to you? My daughter—"

"Do you want a gag, you fool? Your daughter was to marry me, when you stopped it. You stole a fortune in diamonds from me, damn you! And you can sit there and whine that you have done nothing to me!"

"He had nothing to do with my feelings toward you," said Marie wearily. "Blame me for that, if you care to blame anybody but yourself, you beast!"

Breen leered at her, but said nothing. He lighted another cigarette and leaned his elbows on the table. The room was silent now, except for the crackle of the blaze, the soughing of the wind and the dripping of rain outside. A man snored. It was Bill Abelardo, basking in the warmth of the fire.

CHAPTER XVI

BREEN CONFESSES

IT was a long time before Lobo Gomez recovered sufficiently to realizc what had happened. His pig-like eyes finally outgrew their blank stare, he shifted his position a little and looked at Breen. Three feet away from him was one of his own men, crouched against the wall, head sunk forward on his arms.

The Chinaman came in with more wood, and this Mexican shifted his position. No one saw him, nor did they see the brown hand holding a small knife, slip in past Gomez's elbow and quickly cut the rope, which bound the big outlaw's hands. Gomez did not move. Breen looked at him from time to time, but Gomez was in the same position.

Gomez didn't dare move. He realized that Breen would kill him. Gomez had no gun, and the nearest one was a rifle, leaning against the wall, beyond the man who had cut the rope. By the time he could jump up and grab that rifle, Breen would fill him with lead. So Gomez decided to play possum and see how things came out.

There was the faithful Juan, sitting over there beside Maxwell, but Juan was unarmed. He had left his rifle when he went to speak with the two Yaquis along the trail. Time dragged slowly. Gusts of wind caused the old fireplace to smoke badly.

Suddenly there came a sharp knock at the back door. Breen jerked up quickly, and it seemed that every head in the room came up. The Chinaman in the kitchen spoke sharply in Spanish, and they could hear the guard outside reply, although they could not distinguish the words.

"The Padre Demente," said the Chinaman.

"Unbar the door and let him in," growled Breen.

Breen had never seen the mad priest, but had heard him described many times. Still he was hardly prepared for the apparition which came slowly into the house. From the top of his head to his shoulders he was covered with an old gunny sack, filthy in the extreme, with two holes cut for his eyes. Around his shoulders and hanging almost to his knees was an old serape, ragged, soiled. His legs were bare and dirty, his bare feet muddy.

His hands were concealed in the folds of the dirty serape, as he held it close to his body, and Breen slowly backed away, as the priest came into the room, shuffling slowly.

"God, what a mess!" grunted Breen in English, as he halted at the table, staring.

The priest said nothing, but it seemed as

though the eyes behind the sacking were scanning the room.

"Well, Padre," said Breen, breaking the silence, "you are welcome, although God knows I do not care to be married by gunny-sack face. Take that damn thing off! Say something! Here—have a drink!"

He grasped a bottle and shoved it toward the priest, who made no move to accept it.

"Very well," grunted Breen. He turned to Marie. "Get up."

As Marie started to get to her feet, Gomez acted. Breen's back was turned, and Gomez got that rifle. In a second he was on his feet, the muzzle of it covering Breen's back. A sharp cry from Juanita caused Breen to turn.

"Now—your prayer!" said Gomez. "The tables turned, and this time I kill you, Breen. Quick— your prayer!"

Swiftly the priest stepped out of line, a hand whipped from beneath the dirty serape, and a heavy revolver thundered in the smoky room. Gomez dropped the rifle and was falling back, when the priest crashed into Breen, knocking him to the floor. But Breen was no quitter. They came up together, crashing down almost into Marie and her father. The Mexicans were on their feet, but none made any move to assist Breen; none would put a violent hand on a priest.

The fighters fell apart again, scrambled to their feet. Breen tried to back away and draw his gun, but the priest was into him again, locking his arms tightly. This time Breen went down, striking his head against the hard-packed adobe floor so hard that he went limp.

The priest got slowly to his feet, his breast heaving, and looked around.

"If there's anybody around here that's got a spare pair of pants, I'd like to borrow 'em," he said, panting a little, and with a sweep of his left hand he jerked off his head covering.

Marie screamed weakly as the lamplight flashed on Brick Davidson's red hair, but the rest of them were dumb. Brick was hunched forward, his six-shooter tensed at his hip.

"Chinaman," said Brick slowly, "you sabe English. Go and unbar that back door."

Without a change of expression the Chinaman unbarred the door, and in came Silent, Johnny, and Mahan, almost falling over each other. They were wet as drowned rats. Johnny was carrying Brick's clothes under one arm. Juanita was standing up, and Silent swept her off her feet in his first rush.

Johnny and Marie were close together, looking at each other.

"If you ain't goin' to do nothin' but stare at her, yuh might as well give me my pants," said Brick. "Mahan, watch this snake until I get my pants on, will yuh?" pointing at Breen, who was recovering. "Better take the ropes off the folks and tie him tight."

Brick grabbed his clothes and went into the kitchen, where he soon donned his own clothes. Every one in the room was trying to talk at the same time. The prisoners were cut loose, even the Pico and Abelardo brothers. Gomez would never be a menace to anybody again.

Breen knew what had happened. He scowled at Brick, when they sat him up in a chair, but said nothing, while Maxwell told the boys what had happened in there, and of the raid of the rancho.

"We shore was stuck," said Brick. "Mahan knew we never could smash those doors, and that there were guards at each door. We didn't want to start anythin', 'cause it might react on you folks. Our only chance to get in here was to outsmart Breen and Gomez.

"It shore was a blank outlook, until this Mexican Felipe came, pawing around in the dark, tryin' to saddle a horse. We hopped on him good and plenty, y'betcha. He knowed Mahan pretty well, and after a little coaxin' he told us where he was goin'. Mahan had seen this crazy priest, and he knew how he dressed.

"I reckon Felipe was kinda disgusted with Gomez, and decided to play the game with us, if we'd let him off on the raid. We had to time things right, and we shore sweat blood out there not knowin' just what might be goin' on in here.

"Then Felipe showed that he was on the square. He called his name to the guard, and talked with him, while we sneaked in and cooled off the guard. The rest of it was what you saw."

"Another moment, and Gomez would have killed Breen," said Maxwell.

"And ruined things for me," grinned Brick. "I could have bent a gun over Breen's head, and never taken a chance on him, but I wanted him alive."

Breen looked groggily at Brick. "Wanted me alive, eh?" he gritted.

"Yeah—alive, you rattler! I'm goin' to take you back to Montana and hang you for the murder of Scotty McKee."

Breen laughed derisively. "See if you can convict me of it!"

"I'll bet he can!" snorted Ed Pico. "I happen to know that McKee was one of your gang, Breen. You thought he beat you out of a valuable cargo, didn't you? Well, I got that cargo myself. Like a fool, you sent word to McKee that you were going to kill him. He sold out to me, and headed north. But you found out where he was, went clear up there, and tried to make him give back the money. And when he didn't have it to give you—you killed him."

Breen's lips tightened and his eyes gleamed their hate at Pico.

"This is Mexico," he said. "You can't take me out of here."

Brick put his hand on Breen's shoulder.

"Mexico ain't got a thing to do with this," he said. "You can take yore choice. We can turn yuh over to the sheriff at Sicomoro, charge yuh with murder, raiding, and kidnapping, or I can take yuh back to Montana and try yuh for the murder of Scotty McKee. I doubt if you'd ever come to trial down here. Take a look around and see the witnesses against yuh."

Breen wet his lips. "Well," he said slowly, "what do you want me to do?"

"Confess right now to the murder of Scotty McKee."

Breen hesitated. Still, anything would be better than what they might do to him for what he had done that night. They knew he had hired Gomez to make the raid. Even Gomez's men would swear to that.

"I confess to that murder," he said. "I killed Scotty McKee. He double-crossed me, and I killed him."

"When we get to the rancho, you'll put that in writin', Breen."

"Yes. But you've got to protect me."

"These people will keep silent about you, until I get you away."

The Mexicans helped them saddle the horses, and no doubt they were glad to see the gringoes ride away. It left them free to use the tequila.

Mahan rode with Brick and Maxwell to the Border. Mahan was not bashful. He gave them a resumé of his crimes, and Maxwell promised to use his influence to bring Mahan back to good standing. Mahan didn't tell Maxwell that he came to the rancho to try and force Breen to give up the diamonds, and Silent would never tell that part. Anyway, Silent was too busy, talking with Juanita, to care what was said or done.

It was daylight when they rode in at the Rancho del Rosa, where they found the sheriff, deputy sheriff, and the two men of the Border Patrol. Slim had recovered sufficiently to ride and had gone to Sicomoro, looking for help. He had a faint recollection of Brick and Johnny having been at the rancho, but it was too much like a dream. They had only been at the rancho a short time, when the cavalcade came in sight, and Slim was the first one to reach them.

Breen was their only prisoner, and the sheriff wanted to take charge of him, but Brick objected.

"I've got him for a murder in Montana," said Brick. "He's confessed before all these folks, and promised to write it out in detail here at this place. He killed the man that Slade was accused of murderin'."

Breen had nothing to say. He was roped to his saddle, and his horse was being led by Buck Eads, who said he was "jist dyin' for Breen to make a break."

275

Buck's mouth was still sore from that gag. They rode into the patio and began dismounting. The sheriff was anxious to get the details of what had been done, but it seemed as though everybody was too worn out to talk with him.

Buck dismounted and accidentally dropped the lead rope. Breen was watching for any slip that might be made, and the rope had no more than touched the ground when Breen jabbed the horse with his heels, let out a yelp, and the animal dashed for the east arch.

Silent made a grab for the rope, but the horse struck him, sending him spinning. And then the horse and rider disappeared around the corner. Brick was into his saddle, with the horse almost on the run, and narrowly escaped smashing into the side of the arch.

Breen was playing in luck for the moment. His horse had headed south, and luckily the lead rope had roped around one of the stirrups. Breen was leaning forward, urging the horse with short jabs of his heels and an assortment of profanity, when Brick's sorrel settled down to the job. Brick's rope was out, the loop swinging out behind him, as they went crashing down the long slope.

The sorrel was a cow-horse, nosing right in after Breen's horse, running at top speed. Then the loop went singing, dropping over the horse's head, and Brick took a quick dally around the horn of his saddle.

There was nothing delicate in Brick's work. He wanted to stop Breen, and he wanted to stop him right now. The horse whirled off its feet, jerked completely around, and went crashing down in a mass of sagebrush. Brick was down and running along the rope, before the sheriff, Buck Eads, and Berry, the Government man, arrived.

Breen was unhurt, except in spirit, and he cursed Brick from every angle, while Brick unroped him from the saddle. The sheriff took Breen by the arm, while Brick ran back to slacken his rope from the saddle-horn.

He stopped beside the sorrel and looked at his saddle, the fork of which seemed to have upset, pulling the saddle out of shape. It was something he had never seen happen to a saddle. The horn was sticking straight out, the leather stretched to the breaking point from the pull of the rope.

Brick drew out his knife, opened it quickly, and slashed along the leather, which ripped under the sharp blade. The sorrel jerked back, when horn and rope flipped loose. Berry was coming toward Brick, while Buck helped the sheriff to take care of Breen.

The loose end of a piece of cloth flapped from the torn fork of the saddle, and Brick made a quick examination. It proved to be a soft cloth bag, which seemed to have been built into the fork of the saddle.

"By the horn of the moon!" exploded Brick. "C'mere, Berry!"

He cut open the bag, took one look, and jumped down.

"Hang onto that horse!" he exclaimed, and went running to the sheriff's horse, which he almost mounted on the run.

The sheriff yelled at him, but Brick did not stop. Berry was already in Brick's saddle, pawing at the broken fork, trying to dislodge the cloth bag.

"Diamonds!" he yelled at the puzzled sheriff.

Brick dismounted on the run, digging his heels in the dirt, while the crowd at the gate watched and wondered why he came back so fast. They had seen him capture Breen.

Brick's jaw was set tightly, as he stepped up to Joe Pico, whipped out a gun, and poked it at Pico's waist-line.

"Stick 'em up!" he barked, and Joe obeyed quickly.

"I arrest you for the murder of Dell Harper!" snapped Brick.

Joe's face went white, and his eyes shifted nervously. The sheriff rode up quickly, wondering what it was all about.

"You shore was a fool to steal that saddle," said Brick, as the sheriff stepped in beside him.

"What's it all about?" asked the sheriff.

"The day I came here," said Brick, "remember

I won a horse and saddle from Joe Pico? Joe Pico shot Dell Harper that day, and took Dell's saddle. Dell Harper was smugglin' diamonds. The fork of that saddle is holler. Mebby there's diamonds inside the cantle."

"What diamonds?" queried the mystified sheriff. He didn't know anything about smuggled diamonds. Brick rubbed his chin thoughtfully.

"Dell Harper was a smuggler," he said slowly. "I reckon he was in cahoots with a gang across the Border."

The sheriff turned to Joe. "Did you know Dell Harper had diamonds with him, Joe?"

Joe grimaced disgustedly. "Do you think I'd have gambled off that saddle, if I had known? I didn't know anything about it. Harper and I have never been friends. I saw him in Gomez Springs that day, and we met again up here. I asked him where he got that saddle, and he said he just bought it in Gomez Springs from old man Beeman.

"We got to arguin' about things, and he called me a damn hijacker. Harper had been drinking, too. I called him something, and he reached for his gun. I beat him to it, that's all. I guess I was a fool to take that saddle, but I liked the looks of it. I threw my saddle in the brush, and took his. It was self-defense, but I couldn't prove it."

Buck had a death grip on Breen, who made no

comments. Berry had the sack loose now, and he was just a little puzzled as to what to do.

"Here's a fortune in diamonds," he said, "but I'll have to confiscate them."

"And I've been settin' on 'em all this time," wailed Brick. "Well, it's all right with me. As far as Pico is concerned, I reckon the law will give him an even break, because he killed a smuggler, and he says it was self-defense."

"It sure was," said Joe, growing a little easier.

"He's sure toff jeeger," said Bill Abelardo.

"Who—Joe?" asked Al.

"Not Joe—de radhad."

"How about putting Breen in my jail for tonight?" asked the sheriff. "You've got to notify your county."

"I'll go with yuh," said Brick. "That party is worth a lot to me. He can write his confession in the jail."

Brick saw Breen locked safely in the jail, and then sent a telegram to Harp Harris:

WIRE AUTHORITY AND TRANSPORTATION FOR ME TO BRING BACK MURDERER OF SCOTTY MCKEE STOP NAME IS JIM BREEN AND HAS CONFESSED STOP SILENT SLADE WILL COME BACK WITH ME BRINGING HIS OWN PRISONER BUT HE DON'T NEED ANY HANDCUFFS.

BRICK DAVIDSON

Brick did not go back to the Rancho del Rosa that morning, but took a room at the hotel, where he slept until five o'clock that afternoon. Some one was pounding on the door and he got up to let Johnny Snow, Buck Eads, and Silent Slade into the room. They did a sort of war dance around him.

"Silent is goin' to be married," announced Johnny. "We're goin' to have a weddin' at the rancho, and yo're goin' to be best man, Brick."

"No question about it," grinned Brick.

"And that goes any way yuh want to look at it," declared Silent. "C'mon down, Brick; the girls are downstairs, waitin' for yuh."

Marie met him at the foot of the stairs and held out both hands. The rest of them moved over by the doorway.

"Brick Davidson," she said softly, blinking back the tears, "I can't say anything. Dad has found that the mortgage never was recorded. Everything has turned out for the best—even the diamonds are in the proper hands. Dad can't thank you. He told me that he couldn't even talk to you—there's so much to thank you for."

"Well, I enjoyed the little party," smiled Brick. "Everythin' is all right again, Marie. Give Johnny a lot of credit for helpin' put the thing over. He tells me that Silent and Juanita are goin' to be married at the rancho."

"Oh, isn't that wonderful!"

"Why don'tcha make it a double one? I know danged well Johnny—"

"Don't, Brick!"

"Oh, I'm shore sorry, Marie. I reckon I spoke out of turn."

"It isn't that so much. But don't you see, he—he's never—well, I don't know where in the world you ever got that idea. I've never had a hint of such a thing."

Marie's eyes were sparkling, but her cheeks flushed deeply.

"Gosh, I reckon that's right!" exclaimed Brick. "I've shore kept that boy awful busy lately. Well, I'll tell him that from now on—"

"You will tell him nothing, Brick Davidson."

"No-o-o?"

"Who do you think he is—Miles Standish?"

"Miles—oh, yea-a-ah!" Brick chuckled deeply. "Why don'tcha speak for yourself, John? Oh, yea-a-ah. Well, I'll tell him. Sa-a-ay! You wasn't meanin'—me?"

Marie looked up at him, her eyes clouding quickly.

"Brick, I'm sorry," she said softly. "I like you so well, and you've done so much for us."

"Well, now don'tcha feel sorry. Gosh, I thought for a minute I was goin' to hurt yore feelin's. It's all fine, little woman."

"Brick," called Silent. "Here's a telegram for

yuh. Been here at the desk since noon, but they wouldn't wake yuh up."

Brick tore it open and read the message:

WIRING PLENTY TRANSPORTATION BUT YOU'LL HAVE TO USE YOUR OWN AUTHORITY STOP SOAPY SAID YOU'D DO IT AND HURRAH FOR YOU STOP NEXT TIME YOU WANT TO RESIGN A JOB PLEASE SIGN YOUR NAME TO IT STOP ALL OF SUN DOG WAITING

HARP HARRIS, ACTING SHERIFF

Brick read it over twice, a puzzled expression in his eyes. For the life of him he couldn't remember whether he signed his name to that resignation or not. Soapy was one of the Commissioners, and he was just stubborn enough to block their acceptance, if it wasn't signed.

The sheriff came in, looking for Brick, and Brick showed him the telegram.

"Well, I dunno much what it means, Davidson, but it looks as though things were all right at home. But here's the big piece of luck for you. Do yuh know what them diamonds were worth?"

"I dunno a thing about it," grinned Brick.

"Well, you'll find out. As soon as the value is appraised, you'll get a check from the Revenue Department for twenty-five per cent of the value.

283

One fourth the value belongs to you, you lucky devil."

"Gosh!" breathed Brick. "Talk about luck. Go away broke and disgraced—come back rich and exonerated. Sheriff, it's a good old world, if you've got nerve enough to act foolish."

"I'm still hazy on the whole deal," said the sheriff. "Won't anybody tell me what happened across the Border, it seems. I've asked everybody, and they all tell me to ask you. Who and what in the devil are you, anyway?"

"Me?" grinned Brick. "Well, I thought I was just a red-headed trouble-maker, but I find I'm still the sheriff of Sun Dog."

"I can see that by the telegram. C'mere."

He drew Brick aside and lowered his voice.

"Davidson, who was in on that smugglin' deal with Harper? You and me both know that Dell Harper never had money enough to handle this side of the proposition. Who was behind Harper?"

"Well, I'll tell yuh who I think," and Brick whispered one word. The sheriff looked blankly at him, turned slowly and walked outside, where Berry and Mitchell were waiting for him.

"Did he tell you who it was?" asked Berry in a whisper.

The sheriff nodded slowly, rubbing his stubbled chin.

"Yea-a-ah, he said it prob'ly was the Devil."

Berry nodded gravely. "That won't hardly satisfy the Revenue Department; so I'll say that Harper was the man, and let it go at that."

"And it can't hurt Harper," said the sheriff. "I was told to invite you boys to the weddin' at the Rancho del Rosa to-night. Slade and the McKee girl."

"Are yuh sure they want us?" asked Berry.

"I hope to tell yuh, they do. Why, they've even invited Ed Pico and the Abelardo boys."

"Well," laughed Berry, "under those circumstances, I reckon we can leave the Border unguarded for the evenin'."

And they all came. Bill and Al wore white collars and almost choked to death. Brick was best man, and he stood very straight and solemn beside Marie during the ceremony. It was the Abelardos' first wedding ceremony, and they didn't seem to appreciate the solemnity of it all. Perhaps they thought it was Brick's wedding. At any rate, as the minister prayed over them, Bill thought out loud.

"He's sure toff jeeger all right."

"Sure," agreed Al, "theese radhad ees mucho malo—damn good hombre."

Which took much of the solemnity away from the wedding, but did not make it any the less binding. After the ceremony, Maxwell took Brick aside, while the rest of them filed into the dining-room.

"You are going to leave us?" he asked.

"Oh, sure," smiled Brick. "I've got to go back home, Maxwell."

"I know; I've talked with Juanita. God knows, I wish you luck, Brick. And if things ever break badly for you, don't forget that anything and everything on the Rancho del Rosa is yours for the asking. Slim says he is going back to Arizona; so I am making Johnny Snow foreman, and giving him a share in the rancho. Marie said it would please you, because you like Johnny so well."

"Please me?" Brick looked through the dining-room door, where the guests were being seated. Johnny and Marie were near the door, heads not over a few inches apart, as they talked.

"You know I'd do anything to please you, Brick," said Maxwell.

Brick turned and looked at him, and they smiled at each other in mutual understanding.

"Thank yuh," said Brick. "I hope Johnny appreciates it."

Center Point Large Print
600 Brooks Road / PO Box 1
Thorndike ME 04986-0001 USA

(207) 568-3717

US & Canada:
1 800 929-9108
www.centerpointlargeprint.com

1-13